# My Brahmin Days

### and other stories

## Cyril Dabydeen

**TSAR**
Toronto

We acknowledge the support of the Canada Council for the Arts for our publishing program. We also acknowledge support from the Ontario Arts Council.

"Marrying an American" was published previously as "Something to Talk About" in *Journal of South Asian Review* (Michigan, 1982); "Christmas," in *Caribbean Short Stories: I See These Islands* (Germany: Langenscheidt-Longman, 1995), and as "Masquerade," in *The Globe and Mail* (24 December 1991); "Burning Wood" in *Kairos* (No. 9, 1997); and "Going to Guyana" in *Jahaji* (Toronto: TSAR, 2000).

Canadian Cataloguing in Publication Data

Dabydeen, Cyril, date
    My Brahmin days: and other stories

ISBN 0-920661-85-8

I. Title.

PS8557.A25M9 2000        813'.54        C00-932123-3
PR9199.3.D32M9 2000

Printed in Canada by Coach House Printing.

TSAR Publications
P. O. Box 6996, Station A
Toronto, Ontario  M5W 1X7
Canada

*The past is a foreign country.*
*They do things differently there.*

L P HARTLEY, *The Go Between*

# Contents

# Burning Wood

I looked out the window as the aircraft whirred, hummed. And the thought came to me: *No trees*! I rubbed my eyes, my nose pressed flat against the window. The ground moving closer, and Canada had no trees. The austere old woman sitting next to me kept looking over my shoulder as we continued flying into no-man's-land: barrenness, emptiness.

My moment of resurgent memory: Wait until I tell Tomlinson this, I thought, against the plane's louder noise. The old woman grimaced, confirming my fears just then.

Tomlinson, I figured, he'd simply laugh. Good old Tomlinson, the Ojibwa: he and I planting all those trees not so long ago in the forest, weeks at a time, and the blackflies and mosquitoes were God-awful, so plentiful.

Tomlinson laughed and kept calling out the names of trees. He pulled out another bundle of seedlings from the bag hunched across his back, laughing harder. Floating Feather: he simply made the name up. Laughing again, despite blackflies and mosquitoes swarming.

"Just don't think about the insects," he hollered. "Yeah, you're wondering how come I have such a name—Tomlinson. Strange for

*1*

an Indian to have such a name, no?" A wide grin gashed his face.

He looked up at the woodpeckers rat-tatting away, drilling holes into beech bark. Tomlinson pointed and said, "See, it was my father's name. Yeah, Tomlinson. Such a name, with the men, women, children all laughing at him. Yeah, my father was a proud man, he kept his name. Maybe my mother wasn't Indian at all, wasn't Cree or Ojibwa." He kicked up flecks of dirt, muttering, "Sometimes he remained quiet, see." Tomlinson growled, something boiling in him.

"Is that why you keep giving the trees names?"

He resumed planting, scuffing the topsoil with almost worn boots. He bent down quickly, planting the next tree in one quick but smooth motion, tugging it to make sure the roots were firm in the soil. I'd pattern my planting after his. And there was no need to replant any of our trees, as the crew bosses said.

After going full steam for an hour, Tomlinson breathed hard and wiped a patch of sweat from his forehead. I pointed to a new set of trees, which I hadn't seen before.

Tomlinson squinted; he too hadn't seen these before. And we were in a new area, as I pointed to other trees. His arms seemed to extend in a wide sweep now, taking in all the trees, and he whispered a name or two: trees with burrs on their leaves. Healers, he called them, his voice low; and he didn't want anyone to hear him now. Only me. Insects singing a dirge and wail about his face.

Then, "Firs they are. Every goddam one of them are," he cried. "Yeah, never mind what I call them." He stamped on the ground.

I looked at the sack across his shoulder: so quickly he was getting rid of its contents. He was the fastest planter among us, which I overheard the Camp Superintendent say. Tomlinson stood back and smiled, as if I was in on some secret with him. He winked, as my mind raced with new thoughts. The flies becoming really bothersome now as Tomlinson slapped hard at them. Then, pow-pow-pow. Sounds bursting in my ears.

Tomlinson turned around, agitated, angry. Hunters were about, and maybe we'd get our backsides shot. "This is Indian forest, damn it!"

Then he started laughing, as if he'd orchestrated this. Pow-pow-pow. More of breaking branches and scattering flat grass, then Tomlinson pretended being shot dead, collapsing on the ground, Mother Earth! Eyes closed, the entire forest humming, bears dancing in the sky above.

"Get up, Tomlinson," I said. A whole forest dying in him now, I sensed. "Eh?"

In his eyes the invisible eagle flying. Other animals, the moose, wild ducks, geese, a partridge limply hopping for cover in the shaded dark in this Nipigon district.

*

Tomlinson again laughed, pointing with a makeshift gun . . . and an eagle kept falling to the ground. The sky dying, more than a winged death. The nearby lake water now still, despite a loon starting to cry. Tomlinson's mouth opened wide, his eyes making strange turns in a hoodwinking time. More bullets whizzing past. "They will shoot us in the backside as we plant again," he cried, making deliberate Big Foot strides, evolution before my eyes. Marking this bloodspot-and-cambium life, he was; the horizon wavering.

Tomlinson said, "This forest is sacred. Our ancestors' spirits are alive, they're all here. All the dead animals hunted in the past are also here. Their voices here too, yeah, no matter if all the trees are firs."

His heart beating faster in the bramble bush of pain, ancestry. A furrowed forehead as he stood before me, hands waving. Then he was on a horse racing through the forest, wild eyed. Then he was moose, bear, scampering on all fours. Next he was leaping up to the sky and commanding it to come down to the welcome-unwelcoming earth.

I told him to calm down, please.

"The hunters are here, chum. Soon they'll start cutting down the fucking trees. Each tree trunk is a brain. Yeah, d'you know what the trees are thinking?" He looked pained, fists clenched, ready to scream at the hunters and to catch their bullets if necessary, inhaling their fire power—breath by living breath with a steel-hard tongue.

Round his eyes, a great sorrow overwhelming: all the reservation's struggles, fights with the RCMP; the pain of brothers and sisters, drunk fathers, whoring mothers, others mindlessly committing suicide.

Tomlinson's eye popping out, as he cried, "They will shoot us, I tell you." His teeth chattering, nerves like tightrope . . . and who was the prey . . . the stalker? Tomlinson simmered down, looking at me as if I were an odd insect. Maybe he was thinking of a half-dead, writhing animal: a moose with blood leaking out on the ground and eventually forming roots. An image of knives, axes, always de-antlering of an animal.

I continued planting silently, imagining Tomlinson nursing a grandfather adorned with horns that were really elongated ears. And feather floating in the wind, all in my mind's eye. Ah, Tomlinson was his old self again as he drew closer to me, whispering that we were blood brothers—that was all.

Now where was the old woman in the plane? Where had she disappeared to?

The plane still humming, beating like a giant heart.

Palpitating.

*

Another planting season, and I looked forward to meeting Tomlinson in each burnt-out charcoal-layered, sometimes soggy ground. The smell of the forest deep in my nostrils, the senses with balsam, spruce, pine.

Tomlinson appeared now, he was laconic, reticent. I knew at once something was the matter: maybe he wanted to tell me he was no longer the Tomlinson of old. He pointed to the ash, foul soot swept up in a strong wind. A smouldering fire rising, in lurid tongues. He sat down next to me, as I looked into his eyes. "No, " I didn't want to hear more. Then, "What's the matter, Tomlinson?"

"We shouldn't have come back here, Tom," I added. "Maybe we should be in a bar in Longlac or Sioux Lookout." I was angry with him. And he wasn't just Tom anymore—but TOMLINSON.

He looked away from me, kicking up dust.

"I can't plant here any longer," he said.

4

"Why not?"

"Not any more, mate." He sounded like an old sailor.

"Stop calling me mate."

He kept on muttering that he couldn't plant anymore. "There shouldn't have been a fire here. This is sacred Indian ground."

"Your ancestors are dead. Gone," I said.

"Dammit, I'm an Ojibwa. Fire, it means much to us, as it does to them." His secret self, ancestors in his veins as he stomped about, Next he was walking like a bear or moose, again pretending, sort of. Then he began laughing, mouth widening as if ready to engulf the entire forest.

"What now, Tomlinson?" I wanted to break the spell.

"I suppose I'm making much of the fire."

"You are."

"They're all started by my people. We start the fucking fire, yeah. My people need the work, and the forest is ours, ha." He scoffed. "Now loggers are here. Maybe we'll simply fight the fire in the forest, that's all."

"Or plant the trees?"

He brushed this aside.

"Ha, it's hard for you to understand." He looked pained.

I kept studying him.

"There's no point keeping it a secret any longer. Yeah, I keep asking: why do they cut the trees down? The Abitibi company, why? To make paper to write all those words in Ottawa to keep the Indians down? It's all bullshit, see."

His voice taking on a sharp edge. Right then he called me a foreigner; and what did I understand?

But I told him the forest was mine too. My ploy, defence mechanism sort of. "Work means dignity for my people," he said. Then, "It's why they're buried here, our sacred pact with the ground we're standing on."

I listened to the wind; then it was the sun in his voice. Thunder-claps, lightning. Tomlinson kept on about words written down, treaties since time immemorial, all that his people had signed away, and maybe never did, didn't I know? Standing tall he was, the ground rising. And when he planted again, he pounded the earth with his shovel. Then he dug hard.

Now he seemed to be planting against time itself in swift movements as he tugged at the seedling he carried on his back. Sometimes he looked at one small leaf, tendril, each filament of root a lovely woman's hair, he said. He grunted, wiping sweat from his brows, then sidestepped a muskeg.

I couldn't keep up with him. Yet I was telling Tomlinson of my nightmares, my wanting the fire to stop because I feared they'd burn the whole country down, all of Canada, North America, this Turtle Island!

"Keep on planting, chum," he said, wiping away another ringlet of sweat from his face.

I was too tired to go on.

Tomlinson kept on scolding: Work was all, get on with it! The mosquitoes, blackflies, my face swollen, eyes bloodshot.

Tomlinson hollered, "Get on with it, chum!"

Exhausted, I sat on a boulder and watched him going ahead, the forest all his; while I remained hunched, knees locked with my elbows.

A rainbow forming overhead.

*

"Yeah," Tomlinson muttered as we sat at the edge of the lake not far from the camp: here where we lived a semi-primitive existence.

"What?" I asked.

He had something on his mind, his eyes heavy, a shadow long and grey.

"I will leave."

"What for?"

"I'm finished doing what I've come to do."

I thought back of the day's planting, his frenzied speed, the seedlings shot into the ground like bullets.

6

"I thought you needed the money."

"Christ, I don't belong here," he snapped.

"Where d'you belong, Tomlinson?" I was baiting him, and I figured he was really just a drifter.

He sneered, as if he'd do violence to me. Tomlinson, my blood brother. He muttered again about the wind and the clouds, and the sun, moon; charcoal his face; his forehead ridged.

"I don't belong here."

"The forest is yours, Tomlinson," I argued.

"Stop torturing me." He turned, looking steadfastly into the lake: at the fish below—a sturgeon way down there maybe.

He got up and started walking away from the lake, as if he no longer had a pact with the waves, all that was below.

"Where d'you belong?"

He looked back at me, glaring.

"The trees," I encouraged, "they have to be planted. The ground needs them. You cannot go now."

But he kept walking on. Then he stopped. "You . . . could plant them."

"Me?"

He sucked in air. "You've come here. Now you're not a bloody foreigner on this mother-soil."

"Really?"

He seemed disappointed in my answer. Just then I figured he'd turn back and talk things over.

But he continued on, the ground eating him up. And where was he going?

Back to the reservation to be with his people?

I looked into the lake, at the large ripples, the inevitable sturgeon or pike: what did it matter? All making dizzying, swift turns, then moving sideways, a strong undercurrent pushing everything this way and that no doubt.

The next day I returned to the planting site and worked really hard.

But I didn't have Tomlinson's will, strength or energy, though I felt him prodding me on.

I scoffed at the hard ground, raking the topsoil, scalping it with my hard boots and whipped out another tree from the bag on my shoulder.

I wiped a ringlet of sweat from my eyes.

Then before me, like a miracle—I saw a tree rising up, sprouting from a suddenly generous Mother Earth. Thrilled I was. And I kept on planting, still imagining Tomlinson with me. Yes, he was turning over the ash of burnt trees, stepping over logs, hollow as they seemed after the overnight rain. A voice echoing as I shouted out curses and imagined a bear or moose dogging my steps. Tomlinson, a wide smile on his face; his imprint on the soft ground.

Shadows making spirals on the ground, each a dizzying turn. Next a soaring eagle in Tomlinson's eyes: he was everywhere.

Back at the camp, I was distraught from thinking too much. I went to the water's edge and stood there for a while, hoping I'd see him. A woodpecker's throb in my ears amidst colours, clouds, the sun: all like a great moulting taking place. The lake pulling the sky down, like tarpaulin. Fish and bird one. Feather and scales. The ground's faint but frenzied throb.

"Fooled you, eh?" I heard.

He was behind me. Tomlinson. The whisper of earth, water. Memory that never disappeared.

Nothing ever ended.

\*

The land was truly topsy-turvy, all that I had come to expect. Finally now I was leaving, yet landing. And seeing the lines on the old woman's face I was, as she looked askance at me. "Are . . . there . . . well—no trees in Canada?" I asked.

"All gone, don't you know?"

"But?"

"Young man, where have you been all these years?"

"I was . . . well . . . away." Immediately I thought I was as old as she, yet she called me "young man," with an almost disdainful air.

The plane coming closer to the ground, to the palpable barrenness of landscape; and how I wanted her to tell me more.

But she clamped shut. And I started wondering how long I'd been away from the country. How long indeed?

With a heavy bump the plane hit the ground, bringing me back to reality.

The plane swinging, then rocking. All time's collapse at the water's edge, or an ocean's dreaminess. Disoriented I started becoming. Disembarking.

Then the old woman seemed to suddenly disappear, and I kept looking around for her: she who wasn't really that old after all. She had stepped away quickly.

I hurried after her and still wished someone to tell me what had happened in Canada all these years. Who would tell me?

I began breaking out in a heavy sweat and figured Canada perhaps wasn't where I belonged. So many years had passed, inevitably bringing change.

But I was being pushed by others, everyone hurrying, going somewhere. Pushing me harder, even as I stood my ground.

And all the while I kept looking out for her, this woman. Ahead of me, someone waved. Who?

He drew closer. Shaggy beard, unkempt, smelly, and I could tell. Tomlinson! Here, before me, finally, he who I thought no longer existed: who had simply been a figment of my overactive imagination all along. Maybe. His wrinkled face and skin, yet he looked strong as he stood before me. The word "mate" on his lips. He was ready to start smiling.

He took my bags, and I could tell he was excited to see me.

"I'm glad you're back," he said, grinning.

He no longer looked like an Ojibwa, as if he'd been away from the reservation far too long. And he knew I'd come back to Canada—he really did.

I started thinking of the names of the trees just as he'd once told them to me, each cluster and grove, now spelling them out in my mind.

He knew what I was thinking, same as before. Now he'd explain in detail about each one, a secret he'd kept from me all these years.

"Nothing has changed," he said, still smiling.

"I don't believe you." I was thinking of the old woman again.

"Nothing, but only you perhaps."

I kept looking for the old woman who, I figured, was waiting for me to catch up to her.

Tomlinson still smiling. Nothing had changed, he repeated.

Then a slight nod: acknowledgement of a past, his mute communication.

How I longed to hear more.

The old woman, a few yards ahead, waving to me, her face radiant. Clapping her hands, she beckoned. And I figured that she and Tomlinson knew each other from somewhere. Maybe. Tomlinson was laughing. And did he call her mother?

I rubbed my eyes, noting the resemblance. And Tomlinson blinked in quick succession. His mother coming closer, calling him by his name. His Ojibwa name. A crimson glow on her face.

"See, it's all the same," she began saying, putting her arms about him, jewels of feather about him. And I wasn't sure about what country I was really in, even about the trees we had planted, or how tall they were, or how deeply  buried in the ground under charcoal they were too. And all these trees with strange names, none of which I could remember—ever again.

# My Brahmin Days

In a way I wanted to be more than psychologically prepared for it, as I arrived in Delhi; and Dr Kumar, with his driver, was on time, waiting for me, after my flight from Bombay. He welcomed me with his usual friendliness, zest, the same as I'd seen in him before. His wife and other members of his family I would meet later; and no doubt the latter would be curious about me, as I would be about them, since family was everything in an Indian setting; in Canada too, where I'd been listening to the radio talk shows and reading the newspapers about changing family values.

Dr Kumar kept talking on the drive to his home, on the outskirts of the capital city, and instinctively I began thinking of Jawaharlal Nehru and the Indian struggle for independence: all who'd walked this route, then recreating the Congress Party speeches given in Parliament. Nehru's handsome features I conjured up also, in the period just after 1947: he, boldly walking with Lord Mountbatten (and with Lady Mountbatten, his close friend). Next, Nehru visiting Ottawa and addressing the Canadian Parliament—long before I'd arrived in Ottawa and made it my home; but I'd looked at news clippings, all filled with echoes of a new consciousness and pride. And Mahatma Gandhi, always in one's mental foreground, before me.

Indira Gandhi and other prime ministers I conjured up; and then the Bharata Janata Party making the headlines: all in the subcontinent's steadily changing pace, Hindu orthodoxy mixed with Indian self-confidence on the rise. And the Ayodhya Mosque incident, with not unexpected Hindu-Muslim clashes, heated rhetoric invariably in the air. In a wistful moment, Dr Kumar had told me that in India you had to shut your mind off certain things, it was the only way to survive.

Yes, he'd visited Canada, too—he liked boasting about it—so clean everything was there, the sense of unending space, the Great White North. He was deferring to me. And indeed in India people clustered about you, with space having a different meaning. He laughed, a genuinely tolerant man he was, yet as if he didn't mean what he said. He was an expert on reclaiming buildings, he went around Delhi and the outskirts to look at old structures in existence since the time of the Moguls, bent on "saving them."

But Dr Kumar was given to moments of silence also, like ennui. Now it was a welcoming that I wanted, to ease my anxiety, and he obliged. We arrived at his home, as I kept thinking that everything had to do with family. Mrs Kumar, a little heavyset, looked me up and down and greeted me.

With her I immediately sensed that it had to do with who I was, where I'd been born, and where I'd been living these last twenty-five years. This was the first time she was meeting me. While Dr Kumar started being busy with his fax machine, sending or receiving messages from one client or another, I remained with Mrs Kumar for her to continue the welcome. I mused that so far e-mail wasn't always easy for middle-class Indians, as someone had said to me, because servants did most of the typing. It was just a convenient way of getting things done. "Come here, go there"—silently obeyed, with furtive eyes looking back at one. I was still a newcomer, wrestling with my outsider-insider status.

Mrs Kumar kept seeing me as someone from "far away"—as she

might have described me to her friends on the phone. Words said now with an unaccustomed stiffness, as she became more curious about me, about my Canadian background; and what links did I have with the past? In India I'd often been asked, Where do you come from? Meaning, which part did my ancestors come from in India: a truly multifarious land, with every 500 km the language changing, and much cultural mixing. Imagine bhajans sung in a mosque, I'd been told. India's 5000 years of churning languages, cultures. Mrs Kumar muttered something.

I nodded.

Yes, I was associated with "Indian diaspora." Words whirring; and now I'd come to the "homeland," and Canada suddenly seemed like another planet. Then my South American origins, too: it was mind-boggling.

Ashok (Dr Kumar) smiled, as if he sensed what was going through me.

Maybe he winked at me. Did he really? And would he again tell the story of when he'd first come to Canada? A story he liked telling to his "Canadian" friends, he said, with dramatic flair. Yes, that time about ten years ago when he'd arrived at the Toronto airport on his way to visit an old school chum in Edmonton who was now a Mathematics professor—an Indian who'd made good. And a winter storm was raging across western Canada. Ashok, with a three-hour stopover in Toronto, kept sauntering about the airport lounge, feeling dismayed because he was so far away from home, and what he now saw on TV about the storm. Forlornness overtaking his spirit. Then a tall white man came to him, and asked him where he was going.

Ashok waited before answering, but glad for the man's solicitude. There was no hostility, only concern in the question.

Ashok finally said "Edmonton." Then the man instantly shot back, "Doesn't your family love you?"

Ashok waited.

"Haven't you heard about a blizzard in western Canada?" the man berated, and maybe he figured India was an extremely hot place, and Ashok was here now in the land of deep-freeze. "Your family sent you here, what for? Don't they love you anymore?" the man insisted.

"Love me?" Ashok asked, feebly.

"Yes, to send you all the way to Edmonton, to suffer and die?"

Ashok fidgeted, imagining it to be below forty degrees Celsius every day in all of Canada. How could he survive in such a climate? Ashok laughed many times over as he told this story: really his first encounter with Canada.

Then the man confessed to have never been to Edmonton. When Ashok finally arrived in Edmonton and told his friend Ramraj about it, the latter burst out with guffaws. His friend showed him all the material wealth he'd acquired: a big house, with a TV in every room, and all sorts of ski equipment. Ramraj never stopped emphasizing the ski equipment. Did Ashok actually go skiing with him? From then on, whenever he thought of Canada, Ashok always imagined strong winds, if only coulees, everywhere.

Mrs Kumar listened carefully to some of the Indian words I said: which she silently repeated to herself, the intonation, rhythm, then looked at her husband knowingly. She muttered something to him. Ashok nodding: a recognition, the smattering of old Hindi words, archaisms I used, deliberately. And maybe Ashok was intrigued by his wife's interest in me; both appraising me afresh.

"He's a Brahmin," she finally said, sternly, as if I wasn't there with them.

I looked at them and vaguely nodded. And a Brahmin I would be, though a Brahmin status didn't mean much to me: caste had been thrown out the window a long time ago for us in South America and the Caribbean, and not least in Canada—come to think of it—all in interacting with other races, creeds, and with the passing of time.

"You're Brahmin," Mrs Kumar asserted, unequivocal; there'd be no undercutting her.

I wasn't sure if it was her intuition that made her come to this conclusion, or something else. Visions of being a real Brahmin flitted through me. I'd read somewhere of orthodox Brahmins who, when

*14*

they saw an untouchable coming, would hurry to the opposite side of the street. "It still happens, you know," someone said to me in Bombay. And Dalits in India, almost fifty percent of the population—I'd read about how they were becoming more assertive. And Phoolan Devi, the Bandit Queen, from a low caste was now a member of parliament! All in times of change, of new energies. But now, suddenly with me, time stood still.

Mrs Kumar kept looking at me critically, maybe dwelling on my origins, the indenture past mainly. For her time also stood still. And vaguely I thought—and knew—that Ashok and his wife were Brahmins, Ashok having told me once with a friendly boast. Ah, more stories about Brahminism, like a throwback to earlier times, as I dwelled on an untouchable still being an untouchable, and a Brahmin always a Brahmin . . . and never the twain meeting! Perhaps not indistinguishable from class structure in England.

Ashok had told me about India being the land of paradoxes, which I now recreated in my mind, thinking of partition after independence, then of more recent communal clashes. He'd also mentioned casually of once meeting Prime Minister Rajiv Gandhi, unexpectedly, at Connaught Place, the busy Delhi shopping centre . . . such an ordinary-looking, even a likeable fellow Rajiv was. Ashok laughed; and in the same breath he talked about corruption in government, and of pollution everywhere—each month another five hundred autorickshaws, putt-putt (he called them), were added to the Delhi traffic, emitting more harmful fumes.

I genuinely liked Ashok because of the candid way he expressed himself, yet with a sense of tragedy. He was personally troubled by being Indian? "Here there's greater pollution, maybe as much as in Mexico City," an official from the Canadian High Commission had said to me.

Ashok nodding. And later when we'd stood before the Canadian High Commission—a tall, high building—he'd pointed to the long lines of people, mostly turban-wearing Sikhs—all wanting to get visas—and waving his arms at them, he cried to me, "Look how many people want to come to your country."

"My country?"

I stood on a main street, waiting to cross, but the traffic was bewildering: as if all of India were before me as overcrowded buses hurtled past: men, women, and children hanging out from every angle; and the busyness, chaos, all with horses, cows, a camel, lorries, rickshaws, motorcycles . . . and I couldn't cross to the other side for fear of being run over! And it was the same in other Indian cities. Did the city-planners simply always keep deferring to creeds, religions, with nothing to be discriminated against? India was indeed "God's plenty," someone had said, with the spectacle of it before one's eyes. India impacting on the senses, as I'd stood on the side of the street for more than an hour, while frail- looking women, fearless, hurried across. And I'd been told that moving a cow from the street was an expensive proposition. A crane had to be mobilized to hoist the animal away!

An emaciated-looking woman lifting up a small child before me, importuning for alms. A bedraggled man holding up a bronze cobra with tongue jutting out, also wanting alms.

"Don't give them anything," snapped someone at me.

"Eh?"

"You will only spoil them!"

Brahmin I still was, growing in Mrs Kumar's eyes.

But could a Brahmin have ever gone to the West Indies as an "indentured" labourer, as my forebears were? It puzzled her, and puzzled me too.

Ashok was still busy on the phone, maybe deliberately. Something about an arranged marriage for his daughter, Anjali, he hummed. Yes, I would meet her too, and his son Amit. Soon. Ashok, always with good humour, talking about the latest phone conversation, and something about Canadians' preference for a "love match."

Mrs Kumar still evaluating me, sensing me wrestling with an insider or outsider consciousness, as if I was in a perpetual limbo. Suddenly she let out: "Asians are the smartest people in the world!"

Was she referring to human intelligence? "Really?" Ashok had said to me that his wife was the headmistress of a girls' school specializing in the sciences. "It's just a theory."

"No, it's a fact," Mrs Kumar shot back.

"But . . . ?" I visibly struggled.

"Because of melatonin."

"Melatonin," I muttered, vacantly.

She didn't elaborate: she left it at that; and then I began thinking that in Canada there was a psychology professor, named Phillip Rushton of the University of Western Ontario, who'd postulated a theory of intelligence based on racial types; and in his hierarchy, Asians were on top. A debate had swirled about this, as to whether Asians indeed were the most intelligent people—all of which led to much ridicule in the media, and downright laughter at parties everywhere.

What did Professor Rushton mean by Asians anyway? People of Chinese background, who were called Southeast Asians in Canada? And people from India: they were simply called South Asians. My mind humming . . . thinking the Chinese were now the most populous visible minority group in Canada, most doing well in the social and economic life of the country—some of the best doctors and scientists being of this origin. Some of the best too were of other races, including Africans.

Tell Mrs Kumar this. No, she hadn't heard of Professor Rushton, she said. But by the look she gave me, Ashok gave me too, I figured they knew. Now I was beginning to recognize that Indians were a sociable and adaptable people, with a genuine gift for extracting humor in every situation. And without humour Indians wouldn't survive, I'd been told in Bombay: all the tragedies they faced, including the monsoon onslaught coming from across the Arabian Sea. Before leaving Canada I'd heard an Irish Canadian friend blithely categorize professions according to racial types: Indians were good business people—they could sell you anything. The Chinese and Japanese were good at technical stuff: like computers, and so on. And Africans—especially

African Americans—were good at sport. The British? Well, they were good administrators. The days of the Raj, remember? The Irish indeed had the gift of the gab!

Mrs Kumar had a determined expression, while Ashok once more went to the phone, to discuss an arranged marriage for Anjali. And Mrs Kumar again told me about Indians being the smartest people, because they'd withstood invaders down through the ages: the British and the European powers (French and Portuguese mainly), and before, the Moguls (famous for building the Taj Mahal); and in the fourth century, B C, Alexander the Great had been stopped by Indians from conquering the world. They'd sent him home a broken man, and not long after, he'd died!

Was Mrs Kumar playing up to my apparent deep-seated Brahmin instincts? Was it her way to reclaim me, because I'd been "lost" from the tribe after having been an "indentured labourer" in the South American Caribbean?

Ashok, with the phone hanging from his ears, smiled. And I began thinking I might have been living too long in Canada; yet I kept trying to be sociable, not wanting to disagree with Mrs Kumar: I wanted to be a good house guest, all in my desire to be an insider, in a far land. And maybe meeting their children would help matters, I figured, make things more agreeable.

Would it?


Mrs Kumar's daughter, Anjali, shy, obedient-looking, had been listening to us all along. Her dark eyes with long lashes flitted constantly; and she was the one for whom Ashok was trying to find a suitable groom, in the appropriate arranged-marriage tradition. She was coping with a quiet acceptance of it, I sensed.

Wanting to divert attention away from myself I said to Anjali, "What grade in high school are you?"

She tittered. Mrs Kumar glanced at her daughter.

Ashok did also, and muttered something with a smile. Anjali's eyes flitted again, then she suddenly boasted, "I teach in a college." A gloating laugh followed.

"Oh?" Then, "What do you teach?"

"Electrical engineering," Ashok answered for his daughter. Mrs Kumar's influence, to be sure: all that science, as she began to explain that Anjali's college was one of the best in Delhi, and she taught mostly male students.

I tried to imagine Anjali before her class, shy as she looked, with rowdy male students thumping their desks, as she fretfully let out at them the word *goondas*—louts—in sheer frustration. Then she commanded them to listen to her, teaching them with earnestness, scribbling mathematical equations and symbols on the board, all in a fine hand, as everyone copied it all down. And there would be an exam soon: everything rigorous, mechanically done. The same Anjali for whom Ashok was phoning around for a suitable groom!

And Indians were a truly smart people, I tried to indulge Mrs Kumar who was yet eyeing me, a Brahmin as I was, melatonin still in the air.

Ashok again smiled. Let the women—meaning Mrs Kumar and Anjali—talk all they wanted. He kept the phone dangling on his shoulder. And did Mrs Kumar now figure she had the upper hand, she and Anjali: a twosome?

Amit, the son, joined us. Now at least I would have another male on my side.

Tallish, fair-skinned, with soft hands, soft-looking eyes, Amit was home from university because it was Diwali, the special holiday season. In the north of India, Diwali was an important festival, I'd been told: all about Sarswattie, the goddess of light and learning; and in Bombay I'd heard only firecrackers everywhere during this festive season, and was quickly told Diwali was a north Indian festival only. But each time I heard the firecrackers exploding, I thought of an act of terrorism because of imminent war between India and Pakistan. In Delhi, such firecracker explosions added to my anxieties.

I took Amit's outstretched hand of greeting; for me it would be no *pranam*, even though I was Brahmin. He looked like someone filled with piety, he seemed like someone I would get along well with. Ashok still on the phone, haggling.

Mrs Kumar kept her gaze on me, fully. Anjali did the same. Ashok's words, all in Hindi, his jabber, persuasion; and I wanted him also to be on my side, because of my nascent Brahmin anxieties.

Anjali, looking at her mother, sensed my distress and giggled. Or maybe she giggled because of what she overheard on the phone, her father making arrangements to meet a prospective husband for her. Mrs Kumar instantly heaved in. It was her husband's job to make the phone calls, according to the arranged-marriage tradition, a father talking to a prospective father-in-law, man to man. Remember, Indians were the smartest people in the world. Melatonin still in the air.

Anjali glowered. Immediately I thought again of the mostly male students in her class, and the way she seemed to be in command now, wisplike, intriguing me no end.

Mrs Kumar smiled, really for the first time.

Ashok's face still tense. And a viable arrangement was being made, an auspicious time as it was, and my being here, a Brahmin indeed.

Amit, well, he looked around uncomfortably, or seemed bemused.

I expected him to say anything to rebut or even confound notions of superiority. He only looked at me, a little sadly.

Anjali again giggled.

The longer I stayed and kept contemplating, the more I thought of Hinduism and the caste elements, all combined with my own role now in India. Everything Ashok suggested I listened to keenly: this being expected, or inevitable. And Amit gravitated towards me, as if he suspected something else: he who attended university in Nagpur and said he'd studied the prose of Dale Carnegie in his first-year English class (he was an engineering major).

I tried to conjure up Carnegie's *How to Win Friends and Influence People*—one that I'd thumbed through back in Guyana, almost in a prehistorical time. Amit laughed when I told him what I thought. He also glanced at his mother, then at his father, a dutiful son as he was. Family was still all.

Amit was serious, bent in his pious ways. He didn't have his father's congenial manner, cultivated through much socializing no doubt. But Ashok might have encouraged him to get close to me now, thinking something Canadian in me would rub off on him. And maybe Mrs Kumar too wanted Amit to be friendly with me. Because I was a Brahmin also?

All in changing times, in the new India in the making, I considered. Indeed Amit interacting with me, the time being auspicious: there was no need for an astrologer to be consulted.

Amit laughed. Anjali was about to grin again, but her father waved to her, hinting that a match was in the making. Anjali blushed, yet glanced at me.

Then as though to divert me Amit urged that I visit Agra to see the Taj Mahal. Yes, it'd be a way to see how clever Indians really are. Did Mrs Kumar smile? And in Canada whenever I told people I was coming to India, they quickly beamed and said I'd indeed see the famed Taj Mahal—as if wanting me to bring it back with me. And a few Indian friends in Canada had said that most beautiful sites in India were just hype, but not the Taj Mahal!

Amit laughed. He knew I wanted to see the Taj Mahal. He would come along with me, on a bus tour.

Agra was only about 150 km away. Every five kilometers there were temples, Amit pointed out, then began talking about the Hindu epics, as if compelled to. The Vedas mostly, and he knew much about the *Bhagavada Gita*, in the *Mahabharata*, and about the many deities. Emphasis was on Rama (in the *Ramayana*), a manifestation of God in bodily form, the full expression of the triumvirate of Brahma, Vishnu, and Shiva.

Amit becoming serious, solemn, as he took my questions. He went to the temple once a week, every Tuesday, and before important events in his life, such as exams, he read the Vedas. He also allowed the pandit to see his school books at such times, and he would make appropriate prasad offerings. He'd share blessed fruit with others.

Whimsically, I imagined the pandit glancing through the Dale Carnegie text. Yes, *How to Win Friends and Influence People.* Ah, the questionable Brahmin in me, as Amit sensed my indifference, or boredom. He tried another tactic, talking about the ten reincarnations in Hinduism—fish, then narasimha (lion with the face of a human, the sphinx really), and my interest perked up. Then it wavered again.

We were going to Agra, to see the Taj Mahal, Amit reminded me and he laughed, calling it an Indo-Islamic monument. He'd seen it only once, he confessed. In the same breath he went on about Brahmin piety, and the complex hierarchy of castes. Suddenly he laughed again, uncharacteristically.

Then he seemed reminded of his mother's presence, something like it, with us. I recalled Ashok making phone calls in order to find the most suitable boy for Anjali. Yes, the Canadian in me, as Amit now wanted to know about. And just when I thought he would resume his solemn tone and become unbearable, he asked, "Have you been to Woodstock?"

"Woodstock?"

"Yes, you know . . . ?" A beatific grin swept across his angular face.

"No," I said, smiling.

"What about the Rolling Stones, have you seen them?" His tone was eager, unexpected.

When I shook my head, Amit seemed disappointed. He tried next, "How about Pink Floyd?"

My turn to ask questions; and yes, he and his friends at Nagpur University attended movies: they'd recently seen *Jurassic Park.* Who were his favourite Indian movie stars and singers, the Bollywood types?

Sunil Shetty, Aamir Khan, and Sonny Deol, he said.

I looked out the bus window at cow-dung plastered houses, the genuine rural India we were passing yet where large-scale cultivation was being done. I pointed to what seemed like small grain store-houses, and Amit said people lived in them. I immediately thought of caste once more.

We passed more temples on the way, as our conversation focussed on the country's future. Amit telling me all about India's industry: diamond refining and exporting cars, and computer software technology, and there was also food processing and space technology. What about Pakistan, what did he know about it?

He shrugged, dismissing it as a military state, one still coping with feudalism. Was he a member of the BJP, with Hindu resurgence everywhere? He merely said that the British didn't teach Pakistan anything about democracy.

I was suddenly glad as we drew closer to Agra, with taxis, auotrickshaws everywhere. And people selling things. Oddly, I kept thinking of Mrs Kumar, with the Taj Mahal somewhere in the far background. Then an image of Ashok and Anjali having an earnest talk, about "a suitable boy."

I tried to focus on the present: Amit forcing me to it, pointing to the Akbar mausoleum with its special architecture. Akbar—the third Mogul emperor in India, who'd worshiped the sun god. We mingled with the other visitors in this guided tour, caste now far away it seemed as I chatted with the strong-minded, handsome Indian woman from Madras who was home in India after working for the past two years in Uzbekistan as a railroad land surveyor. She insisted that Hindi was the language of the north of India only, not the south; and why should it be the national language? Why not English? Her two beautiful children, boy and girl—nine and ten respectively—speaking a perfectly pitched English seemed like sudden reincarnations of the deities.

Amit kept observing them and me with a smile.

A Seattle couple recently arrived from Kerala said they wanted to know what my faith was. They wanted to keep in touch with me when I returned to Canada. They were on their own missionary journey, I figured. I was yet a Brahmin, didn't they know?

The Taj Mahal, magnificent . . . the Emperor Shah Jehan lifting the veil from his wife Mumtaz Mahal's face, and beholding her radiant beauty, and declaring, "You're like an ornament." Upon her fourteenth child-birth, she'd died, and a mournful Shah Jehan erected his famous monument to commemorate her—one that took 20,000 men working, and which was finished after twenty years, a structure blending Indian, Persian and Islamic styles.

The Taj Mahal's central dome rose seventy-three metres, and the complex covered seventeen hectares. Our Agra tour guide kept on at it, an ex-army man, proud to be a professional and boasting of having served presidents and other VIPs. Yes, former British Prime Minster, James Callaghan—the guide added—whose wife asked him if he would build such a monument for him.

"Only if you bear me fourteen children," Callaghan replied.

Somewhere Mrs Kumar laughing, I heard.

Ashok also laughing. And he was still on the phone, because the last suitor had proven difficult. He told me when I returned from Agra, "The parents agree to the match, but not the boy," and rolled his head.

Anjali quietly sniffing at the arranged-marriage tradition. Her honour had to be kept intact, I assured her, yet her parents' wishes must be obeyed, family still being all.

Amit nodding. Mrs Kumar, not brooking any contrary opinion about Asians being the smartest people.

The ex-army man, the tour guide, responding to my question about why no vandals or terrorists ever attempted to destroy the Taj Mahal due to Hindu-Muslim rivalry. "The Muslim never would, you see," he drummed, "because it is their monument."

Then he added, "The Hindus, well, they don't destroy buildings. They will go for gold and silver, jewellery, you see. But never destroy buildings!"

The magnificent Taj Mahal in my mind, and thinking of returning to Canada with my senses intact, all the while appraising everything afresh because of the photographs I'd taken, in the same spot where Princess Di had stood—said a waiting cameraman eager to snap me again for another two hundred rupees!

Everything would stand the test of time, someone muttered near to me; not just the Taj Mahal, but all of India too which had withstood partition and the factionalism between Hindus and Muslims.

Mrs Kumar fidgety, still believing Asians were the smartest people.

Why now I started frowning, I didn't know. Maybe it was because she no longer thought I was a Brahmin! Amit had briefed her perhaps.

Ashok shook his head after another arduous phone call, and said he'd finally found a suitable boy. Amit again laughing, yet with a sense of piety, the deities in the temple seeming mysteriously to be at his beck and call: all in the land where my ancestors had come from, and I wanted to linger much longer. But my Brahmin days were over, I knew.

Ashok, well, he wanted to regale me once more with going to Edmonton, and enduring the fiercest winter ever.

He would write and tell me a few months later about Anjali and her husband going off to live in Miami, all because of the engineering skills they possessed and were much in demand. Mrs Kumar waving to me and saying, "I told you."

Amit, back at Nagpur University, and rereading his Dale Carnegie text all because of what we'd talked about. I also kept imagining Ashok and his wife wondering about the words I'd used, the remnant Hindi phrases: all I'd picked up from a long time ago, from a grandmother who'd come from a part of India I'd never know. Never really know.

The images coming to me fully in the plane. And winter somewhere, in a far land: Canada, as I yet fought to regain my Brahmin status. Strong winds blowing, I imagined; and maybe someone would now ask me if my family didn't love me, and why didn't I return?

*But to where?*

# Christmas

They came forward, went backward: men with strange-looking faces, chiaroscuroed; the drums beating, flutes playing in this percussive parang; and immediately a time of slavery was being relived. Then rebellion, freedom!

And where was Dada, the old man? Grandmother kept asking.

The dancers' faces painted in vermilion, orange, white: all veritable masks covering dark-and-brown features; and one on stilts kept coming forward, lifting his leg high in the air because he had "powers," he believed, akin to the White-lady, Laang-lady, as we also chanted silently. The White-lady, the repository of jumbie spirits, though she was also truly festive.

"See, watch her good!" a niece shrieked.

"Watch the others too!" someone else sang with rhapsody in his veins.

Yet I kept thinking about the old man, Dada: he was indeed in Grandmother's thoughts, she couldn't fool me. Dada, distinctly wrinkled, seventy years old maybe, was somewhere; and the images kept returning to me amidst the clamour of waves, the Atlantic bordering our narrow, undulating coastal area. More waves washing, as if I was indeed elsewhere, next to Lake Superior in Northwestern Ontario where I'd recently immigrated, thinking I also belonged close to the world's largest lake.

Now, oddly, with rhapsody in my veins I was dragging all of Canada—the Great White North—with me to the tropics. And that first snowfall, remember? A ball of snow thrown into my face, and icicles with arms running down my neck and collar. Next, a real storm, with winds howling like an elephant in distress, would you believe it? Ah, the tropics, more than memory, or simply evoked at will; and again I was asking: "Dada, where are you?"

The drums kept throbbing, parang beating everywhere.

And Grandmother was muttering about my leaving-returning this Christmas, like an omen. The drums still beating, with the masquerade before us, the man on stilts recreating Dahomey's past, or all of Africa in our mixed-race world. And the food being prepared, the seductive or disorienting aromas of pepper-pot: it was Dada's favourite too, I knew, made with cassareep—a special juice or resin from cassava. And black cake or fruit cake, with rum, vanilla. Punch-a-creme. Hazel nuts. Auntie, Grandmother, my absent mother and father, and nieces and nephews—nine of us altogether—running helter-skelter in the house.

Waves surging too, I imagined, against mangrove, courida; then concrete defences had been all, because our houses were built on stilts, though at any moment we expected to face the onslaught of the sea.

"Ha, the Laang-lady!" came the chorus, louder in the sun.

"She is, heh-heh, the same White-lady!" someone sang.

We kept vicariously being everywhere, amidst the louder sounds of drums and whistle, in a veritable concatenation. The men's strides now longer in the sun as we watched as if spellbound, their prancing and doing everything: as if to a special bidding, moving again backward and forward. Some of us were laughing. Dada (Lambert he was, really): an African, distinct in our village, among us who were mainly

East Indians. And he lived alone, sometimes trembling in his ragged boots in his ramshackle house a hundred yards from us.

I would often hear him muttering about a time long past, always his own fervid African memories with a guitar's silent strum in the air. The ghost of a long time ago in his veins, he couldn't fool me. Couldn't fool Grandmother, most of all.

And yet I was back here, still in the Lakehead. Time collapsing, landscapes moving around.

Wait and see.

\*

We looked forward to this time of the year, despite our own determined lore with phagwah or holi, and deepvali with lights flickering: this Calcutta or Bombay with us amidst rhythms of steelband, calypso, reggae. Parang amidst chowtal and bhajan: the energy of our discordant ways as we also determinedly wanted to be ourselves. No other. And yet we wanted apples and grapes, all come from abroad. And was I still somewhere else?

A greater anticipation in me, and in all the other children's faces, as I imagined an apple being peeled. Red-slice, white-slice, and a hand reaching out. Fingers quickly slapped.

Auntie, often surly, broke her silence, saying it was time we put up our own Christmas tree: one that definitely wasn't from the guava or jamun, but which was "foreign-looking." It was from that point on that I started thinking of places beyond our village, with Northwestern Ontario winds somewhere howling in my imagination, and snow drifting, suddenly lifted in the air. A reindeer time too, more than just the imagination because it was indeed Christmas.

Grandmother looked at me, muttering with a strange tongue, with the stamp of indenture on her forehead. And only with Dada, he with thoughts of a fargone slavery, she figured she knew who she was. All I would get to know better in time, maybe.

Dada grimacing, yet with his guitar's forlorn air.

The waves washing again. He would sometimes walk over to our house to start nattering about an imaginary kingdom: Dahomey or

Ashanti, he called it, which he intuitively sensed. Did he? And maybe he belonged to a special religious sect —the same Jordanites I would hear strumming at nights, inspiring awe and fear. Dada with his own guitar hugged to his hips and chest, moths flitting close by, circling him as he played to the entire village it seemed. Crickets metallically cheeping, and all other insects making their presences felt.

Dada soon after laughed, and I remembered him singing a carol, "Silent Night, Holy Night," and with Grandmother he meshed the years, their eyes reflecting the energy of old age, their bones like sapling. His webby skin was like a crocodile's, I thought. He'd once told me he knew people in Canada, America, England: people very different from us because we were from the tropics, all his inner rhythms, talking. Yes, one day I too would go there. And would I become different then?

Would I?

Grandmother's eyes dimmed because of her realization of what was to come, my inevitable departure.

Then, strangely, Dada no longer came to visit.

Grandmother grimaced. She recalled it all for me with a wave of her hand. And Christmas it was now, she kept saying with a sliver of grape on her tongue. Maybe Dada now wanted to be by himself, alone in his house like a prisoner. He might be festering with smells of salted cod, rancid onion. Bread crusted, somewhere. His doors, windows locked, all against the hard sun. No other doors would be opened.

Not now, but for me only, maybe they would open, because I was already living in Canada and knew about Lake Superior.

Grandmother suddenly laughed despite frenzy in her veins, and she said I was always making up things. But she knew I would soon leave, just as Dada sensed; yes, I'd go to a foreign place where it snowed all year round. Why did I want to go there, giving up on the tropical sun itself?

Then Auntie started talking about fancy light bulbs flickering, all now on her "foreign" Christmas tree. Yes, poor as we were. She'd heard that in other places you simply chopped a tree down from some wooded area and set it up. But not here in the tropics.

No one had an answer. We just did what was always done, the past with us being yet a present time.

Grandmother looked out the window where the chickens waywardly scattered, eyeing the magenta-red cockerel: a prized bird, which one of my brothers would take care of. It'd soon be a real feast, a farewell.

Masala and black pepper smells in the air, the pungent curry, and enormous helpings of rice, dhal.

Ginger beer, rum too. Grandmother discreetly swallowing a mouthful, her tongue burning. Appetizer or aperitif! And again the throb of the masquerade drums, a chorus approaching with the cry of White-lady; and maybe she wanted to wave or flutter her hand with a silken handkerchief in the trade wind, as men with madras-coloured shirts, more garish-looking, danced in front of us in our yard, and kept coming closer.

The White-lady indeed coming closer.

All the places abroad coming closer, because of my own ambitions maybe. And how I wanted Dada to see it all.

But he wasn't around.

And I kept being aware of places abroad . . . as we peeped out from windows. Others looking out also at a time when the village and town seemed one because it was Christmas time: such an occasion when all the squabbles and rivalries between the races disappeared as the White-lady lifted a hand, remonstrating with us; the costumed men around her, all willing attendants.

Words whispered. Next payment demanded: penance for all the past wrongs.

We were overawed, spellbound.

And Dada was somewhere also looking out, his guitar's strum in his half-deaf ears. The White-lady lifting one leg higher, arms swinging and advancing.

Stilts being all!

I watched Grandmother go outside, and in mild-mannered obeisance hand a few coins: penance for her own past wrongs. And would she now invite the dancers to come closer, even to enter our house? And maybe it was at that moment I wanted to escape . . . go away to another place . . . close to Lake Superior!

The pot boiling; the ginger beer ready in a large jar which kept it cool and tasty. Vanilla, ice cream churning. The black cake already made, soaked in rum well ahead of time. A whistle blew louder, harder.

Grandmother glanced at me, to see how I was taking it all: for this indeed would be the last time I was participating in these celebrations. Then I'd be gone.

"Come in!" I heard.

Hands to my eyes, I didn't want to see more.

The music, parang indeed, louder.

Grandmother smiled and looked at me.

The White-lady and the other attendants also looking at me, gyrating in a fashion. And fife and drum, the percussion of a long day and night ahead.

Dada, come see, where are you?


Coconut trees wavering alongside the rows of zinc-roofed houses. And everything shrill in our ears. Nieces' and nephews' unending caterwaul, all part of the celebration. Because the White-lady, Laang-lady was near.

*

Christmas morning finally came, with church bells distantly ringing. Everything was ready, the foods we wanted to eat and thought about constantly, cornucopia with our deep longings.

What else? All despite our poverty; and then the paltry gifts we'd present, and it didn't matter, they were gifts nonetheless.

Santa Claus, with advertisement on the radio. Jingles, sing-a-long carols; and maybe my mother would be coming home. And what would she give me, us, this time?

Grandmother mulling over the past, as she always was, and seemed discomfited as she looked at me. The nieces and nephews with rhythms their own: their coming and going all the time in the wind-opened door. Sunflowers and hibiscus on the wayward hedge, wavering in the Atlantic breeze.

"Boy," Grandmother called out, "go and get the old man."

"Eh?"

"Tell him to come now."

She meant Dada of course; she couldn't wait any longer. But I started becoming anxious.

"Go, it's Christmas time," she urged.

"But he wants to be alone, he will not come." Thinking of his cobwebby veins, skin like dried onion in my mind's eye.

"Never mind that," she snapped.

I breathed in hard and started out to find Dada, who was near, and yet faraway. And wasn't I still in Northern Ontario? Chilly winds yet blowing.

A hummingbird acrobatic against the hedge in an emerald haze as I walked down the street, looking for the old man. The others at the window, they'd heard what Grandmother said: Go and get Dada.

A mild chorus now, as they started to jeer because Dada had acquired the status of someone else, a loner or outsider. Drums in the lurid masquerade. Carnival in our blood's constant boil, and voices again like whirring bees. I slowly walked up the rickety stairs of the old man's house, passing the creeping-converging vines, weeds, pushing my way through, the heat overpowering.

The drums silent, yet the cry of White-lady, Laang-lady still in the air.

The final step, the ramshackle boards shifting under my feet as I approached the door. Now I would tumble, fall, as I knocked.

No sound.

Again, knocking. Then waiting.

I heard a noise inside, a guitar's strum, a solitary whine.

He couldn't fool me; he was inside, talking to himself. But what if Dada was long dead—and I was only imagining this? What if Grandmother also knew the old man was dead, yet had sent me to hear him playing for one last time?

I began hurrying down the stairs, almost tumbling. Dada was behind, pushing me along, I felt.

I hurried, faster, to get away!

The others saw me returning, and one yelled: "So where's Dada, eh? He not at home?"

"He gone to America?" another jeered.

"Or is it Canada, same where you want to go?"

"Ah, maybe he gone to his grave!"

Grandmother watching me, and she immediately knew.

It was a time, she indicated, for us to start eating. But she knew something else. Hot curry aromas: sensations of a special kind; the relatives moving about close to the ample rice, spiced potatoes, rotis. And maybe now the White-lady was gone from us, for good.

Yet someone called out that we must listen to the music, muttering about love—the best India would sentimentally offer, brought to us from a gramophone and loudspeaker.

But Grandmother still seemed unlike herself, and she was indeed thinking of Dada, wondering if his relatives—whoever—had taken him away from us.

She looked at me and seemed disappointed because I was unable to bring the old man to us. The gulf between races, hardened beliefs in this creole time, she imagined.

Grandmother shaking her head, No!

I savoured the curry, the pungency in my nostrils.

Auntie scowled in her corner, then motioned to us to start eating.

But Grandmother kept her eyes trained on me. A forlorn spirit taking over despite the gold bracelet on her wrist and the filigreed leaf imprinted on her left nostril. Then she looked around with a wan smile.

Again Auntie urged us on, as she took one Canadian apple—from

British Columbia—and started slicing it near the Christmas tree with multicoloured bulbs. But as I looked at Grandmother again, I figured something was amiss.

I looked outside next. Where was Dada?

Grandmother slowly got up and went to the window, then came back and sat with us, and smiled.

Immediately I knew. I quickly went to the window again. I saw him, leaning on a cane: Dada's familiar figure, in his deliberate style, coming along. "Dada's coming!" I blurted out.

Grandmother got up again, slowly, as if she didn't know what else to do. She smiled, eyes radiant, and she laughed. The others, nieces and nephews, cheered. But Auntie didn't; she kept up a dour expression.

I hurried out to greet the old man. Dada took my hand, gratitude in his eyes, the way he kept smiling, still leaning on his cane, eyes luminous.

A fresh gust of wind, perfumed air, jasmine everywhere. "You came," I muttered, and I wanted to ask him where he had been: had he really been in that house with cobwebs like embroidery, strumming his guitar?

He sat at the table with us, in his best faded grey suit smelling of moth balls.

His eyes caught Grandmother's as the rest of us rattled on about Christmas and faraway places.

Auntie lowered her head, a thin slice of apple in her hand, which she handed to Dada like a peace offering. She rippled with a smile next.

After, Dada took a shot of rum in a small glass and held the glass in his quivering hand. When he swallowed again, his throat bulged, eyes aflame.

It was good, once in a while, he began saying.

And he ate large mouthfuls, eyes bright as he swallowed.

Grandmother laughed again as Dada wiped his mouth; and it was a time for the other delicacies: the special black cake, grapes, another slice of apple.

Suddenly we heard the drums again, the masked men approaching, Dada's guitar now at hand, which he would strum.

Parang: discordant, rousing, everywhere. The White-lady approaching once more, with strange blessings because Dada was indeed with us. Or maybe because they knew I'd be going abroad and would start feeling icy winds blowing across Lake Superior, across all that I would one day want to call my own.

Flutes and whistles, in celebration.

The White-lady's troupe of cheerleaders egged us on. The sun shining brightly everywhere, as Dada kept up his own strumming, his body no longer bent but ramrod straight.

The snow's iridescent hue, with lake-water rising.

My memory of distant places overpowering.

Other images of reindeer too, close up, as I imagined pulling along on a special sled over heavy snow.

. . . Church bells ringing, carols everywhere in a far country, as I sang with others I hardly knew. And somewhere I heard Grandmother's laughter because of Dada's wayward strumming, with voices around us, all that I'd want to hear again, in places everywhere.

# The Cottage

How the weekend was going to turn out preoccupied me in a way. It preoccupied Suzan as well, and she laughed nervously. I sensed she wanted us to be alone. Yet she murmured, "You've never met my Mom, Phil"; and in almost the same breath she began talking about Kingston, the university town where we'd met five years ago. In Montreal now, we were set to head out for the Laurentians. And the old man she'd encountered on the way to Montreal: would he come along with us? Suzan smiled. Gnarled, reeking of tobacco he was: he lived a lonely life on Bagot Street, in Kingston, she said.

She talked wistfully about him like he were an old friend. "You must come and see me when you return, dear," the old man had urged. "I will, I told him." Suzan's promise indeed. "There are many people in Kingston, Phil, who're lonely. Ever thought of these people being everywhere?" She seemed like a new Suzan now.

The bus started out from Montreal—where she'd grown up. Now we were heading for the Laurentians, Suzan having invited me to spend the weekend at the family cottage in St Agathe. (Maybe her sister Brigette—Briggy—might be there.) Suzan's hand was in mine as the bus kept going; and the old man's words came back to me:

"Promise, Suzan, you must come and see me when you return. The students in the rooming house where I live, they party all night." I remembered my own Kingston days at Queen's University. Suzan had attended Queen's too, but gave it up to pursue an alternative lifestyle: she'd grown to distrust the intellectual life. Life of the emotions, the senses and the spirit, was what she wanted. To test out other possibilities, new experiences. The bus rumbled on as apple-cheeked French Canadians entered or exited. A freckle-faced youth hugging his long-haired girlfriend, both carrying knapsacks. The air raw this July, crisp. Undulating roadway, rising hills, the township elongating with ski resorts, more cottages, reminding me of Scotland—two years ago I'd been traveling from Inverness to Edinburgh, from one castle to another. "It's such lovely country here, Phil," Suzan quietly said. "It makes me nostalgic for when I used to come here as a child, going to our cottage. Now this trip seems unbearably long." Reflectiveness marking her face.

I began telling her about Ottawa: the life I lived. Yes, the bureaucracy with its endless paperwork, government shibboleths, rules and regulations; the Minister's speech notes, the civil service's pecking order.

"It's the experience in government that counts, isn't it?" Suzan murmured. What did she mean? She grinned, and was she still thinking about the old man? Surprising moments, all in our on-again, off-again relationship. How much, too, we kept thinking of new possibilities: which this getaway weekend now seemed to offer. The bus trundling along, as she pursed her lips. Yes, she preferred Kingston; and one of that city's poets had said Kingston grew on you the longer you stayed there. Tom Marshall? Kingston, where Founding Father Sir John A Macdonald was buried (we'd visited the cemetery—Suzan and I—on a whim one night after drinking in a bar on Princess Street). But Ottawa had overtaken all that: the political talk swirling, though I'd occasionally remember that cemetery visit.

Three hours it'd take to reach St Agathe, her parents' cottage, Suzan muttered, jolting me back to the present. She hadn't seen her parents—her mother mainly—in quite a while, though they'd talked on the phone, argued more like it.

"It's so different from the Middle East, too," she added, like an afterthought.

That past. "My parents, especially Mom, still hold it against me, you know." For going off alone? "I hope Mom understands things have changed now. Gosh, I still love her. I wish I could make her understand. She loves me too, but she thinks I'm not like her other children. She forgets I'm a grown woman of thirty-five. You know, she used to take care of my hair, braids, curls, as a child; show me off to her friends. You should see the photographs; I remember each one, all the details." She dabbed at her eyes. The bus's insistent rumble, then the increased speed.

Suzan added, "My father, well, he's getting on, too." Downhill again, the ride beginning to seem interminably long. In Suzan's silence, the Middle East, olive trees, Palestine. The warm hospitality of the Arabs she'd met, not so long ago: they were the friendliest people in the world, she'd said. Was that what she'd tell the old man on Bagot Street? She was fixated on him.

Suzan's passion, or rage; and maybe she was hoping life would change for her.

More people entered the bus, making small talk behind us. A thin, wizened-looking woman fingering a rosary, her life of confession sustained in whispers. "It's beautiful here," I casually said. Suzan nodded. "Dad, well," she added, "he was always away from home; he left Mom alone so often you know. He'd go to Brazil, or somewhere else, his work taking him everywhere. And Mom was bored out of her mind being alone with us; then she started drinking."

She hesitated.

"Aren't you being hard on her?" I offered.

"My alternative lifestyle now . . . she doesn't approve." Suzan, one of the children of the middle class going back to the land, wanting to save the planet because of a new ecological interest. Save the environment! "Oh, Phil, it's more than that." Then, "I wish Mom could see things the way I do."

"Give her a chance."

"I've tried."

"On the phone?"

"I wrote letters." She sighed.

"Maybe this weekend she will grow to understand you." Why I said that I didn't know. Would the rest of the family really be there?

"She won't be there," Suzan affirmed.

"Are you sure?"

Hills, lakes around: a map unraveling in my mind's eye; a diorama, spectacular. A youth, eighteen or nineteen, entered the bus with a large harmonica hanging down his thick neck. Immediately I wished I was a teenager again. Suzan also, I could tell, as she smiled. The bus making a quick turn: on road less traveled; each small town now with another passenger entering. Then the rosaried old woman got up to leave, though not without patting Suzan's hand. It was indeed taking longer than I expected to get to St Agathe. "Oh Phil, it's much longer," Suzan muttered.

Then, "You must understand how I used to hate traveling this distance as a child. But my parents insisted on coming to the cottage. Soon after, Dad would go off to Brazil. Sometimes I'd think he indeed wanted to get away from us."

The lake was really wide: and it kept widening the more you looked at it, with the cottage at one end, jutting out almost at an angle in the afternoon's declining sun. Colours kept washing in the Quebec sky. Suzan scribbled something in a journal. When I'd visited her she would read to me from it, and she was now thinking of writing for the local newspaper, *The Whig Standard*. Details in her journal of her Middle East trip, then Europe: all with naivete or innocence and other thoughts she'd shared with a girlfriend, Brenda. She and Brenda were young, then, everything being "fantastic." No more use of condoms: condoms were part of the plastic world, and they were dead-set against it. Ah, the seventies' excitement; and making love to someone on the train somewhere in Europe also, it being "fucking-fantastic." Because he was black? Brenda being coy about it. What about her one special Arab friend, Ali? Suzan had a crush on him. Didn't she?

Mrs Huggan, Suzan's mother, surprisingly welcomed us at the cottage. Pink lipstick, blonde hair, as she immediately seemed to size me up, while Suzan was trying to make me feel at ease. Her mother was indeed here. "Where did you meet?" Mrs Huggan asked.

"Not in the Middle East, Mom. Phil and I traveled separately. We met in a kibbutz much later." She chortled. "Those places we saw together in Spain too, the Alhambra." Suzan recalled something I had long forgotten. Mrs Daisy Huggan made a sick face, yet forced a laugh. Would Suzan tell her mother that I wanted to make love to her on our first date? But then she had still been in love with Ali. God, I could still remember him, her guide at one stretch of her journey.

"Make yourselves at home," Mrs Huggan grated, seeming frail.

"I told you about Phil on the phone, Mom, that we'd be together . . . this weekend." Tentative, a trying out. Did Suzan want to make her mother feel guilty?

"Yes, dear, you did. But we planned on being here too. I should've warned you about it."

Briggy, Suzan's younger sister, entered, hair streaming wet, her lips pursed. She'd been in the lake, in a canoe. "Gosh, Suzan, it's good to see you!" Briggy embraced her sister, then took my hand, her clothes pasted to her body, the jeans, a flimsy T-shirt. I liked her at once. Suzan laughed.

Her mother sulked, a strange tension rising in the air as Briggy kept talking. "Is Mom staying the entire weekend?" asked Suzan, as Mrs Huggan walked off to the patio. "I thought you knew the entire family would be here," Briggy said, removing a ringlet of hair from her eye. "Gosh, Suzan, it'd be good to see everyone again. It was years since we all met as a family. It's Dad's idea, you know; he makes plans on the spur of the moment."

Suzan seemed mildly exasperated, concerned about how I'd take it. Did she really think we would to be here alone? Ah, I was eager to get away from the government, from the Ministry of Finance's bureaucratic-cum-political world. Yes, face up to it, I'd been told. Keep predicting Q's and A's, what would be asked in Parliament: to always prepare for "Question Period."

Briggy chirped, "Bob and Steve are also coming, Suzan. Gosh, it's been such a long time." Bob and Steve: the former, Suzan's baby brother, now seventeen; and Steve—often morose, and unpredictable, Suzan had said. Suzan indeed wished to see her brothers: to see how much they had grown and changed. Mrs Huggan, not wanting to be antisocial—she said—rejoined us. "Your father will arrive shortly. I hope Bob gets here on time too. He's still a baby, you know."

"He isn't, Mom," said Briggy.

"Why would he arrive late?" asked Suzan.

"He's working for Parks and Recreation in Montreal. It's a new job," the older woman said.

"Oh."

A heavy, dull expression took hold of Mrs Huggan's face. The lake water lapping, new rhythms in the clear air also. Raindrops spattering, as Mrs Huggan turned to Suzan. "Are you working now?" Casual, but a directed question.

"Yes, Mom, I do social work."

"Is it the same job you told me about on the phone a month ago, studying low-income workers? Another co-op effort?"

"Yes, Mom." The old man in the bus: was Suzan thinking about him now?

Bagot Street indeed!

"It's not a steady job, is it?" Mrs Huggan complained.

"I don't want a steady job, Mom."

"Why not?"

"We're trying out a new lifestyle."

"Take a course at a college and do something useful, Suzan." Testily said.

"Mom, I just want to live my own life, my way!"

I looked from mother to daughter. Briggy now did a disappearing act to a side room: to change, hair still wet, ringlets about her eyes.

"You aren't getting any younger, Suzan," Mrs Huggan fretted.

"I'm pleased with what I am doing, Mom. Gosh, I didn't want to come, you know. But now I'm here, I guess I have to please you."

"Don't make me feel guilty, Suzan."

"I am not!"

"Your boyfriend's here, let's not quarrel."

"Phil's not  . . . Well, we won't get married, if that's what you're thinking." That look in Suzan's eyes, her moment of embarrassment. Then: "Mom, I'm helping people, real people. I want you to understand that."

"Let's not argue."

*

Colours in the sky, in the clouds. Water lapping noisily, and I inhaled fresh air from the window looking far out across the lake, everything seeming so unreal. Ah, Suzan was getting herself worked up for nothing. I recalled my calls to Suzan from Ottawa. Suzan looking at me. Briggy, where was she? The rain began pouring now. "It's heavenly," Briggy hollered from somewhere. "Do you remember, Suzan, how we used to do that?" Doing what? Being out in the rain?

Steve arrived in an old, battered-looking Buick: a perfunctory smile on his narrow face. After a peck on Suzan's cheek, he nodded to me, then to his mother, before he went to get a power saw. A grating noise rose from where he went. Then Suzan's father arrived, a shortish, heavy-set man, with a small grin on his broad face. "What's it like working in the federal government?" he asked me. Then he turned to his wife. "Why isn't Bob home yet? And where is Steve?"

"Steve's out with the power saw, can't you hear him?" Mrs Huggan rasped.

Bill Huggan cast a glance at me once more. Suzan edged up, closer.

Mrs Huggan muttered: "I don't know why he's not home yet. He should be, that Bob. Maybe . . .

"Maybe what?" barked Mr Huggan.

"He's working late tonight."

"Will he take the train then?" he growled.

*42*

"That's what he said on the phone."

"It'll be after ten before he gets in; and someone will have to pick him up at the station."

"He must have his supper when he gets in," Mrs Huggan fussed.

The power saw ground louder; a lone tree bending, about to come crashing down. Suzan looked at me, then at her father, who stood silent with a Scotch in his hand. Her mother offering me a drink. "So what's the government really like?" pressed Bill Huggan. Words like a refrain. "They should leave Quebec as it is, if you ask me. French Canada will break away anyhow." Why did Mr Huggan really say this?

But he didn't want an answer or an argument, as he sipped his drink. His wife sidled up to him: she seemed languorous, yet pallid-looking in the soft light. All so deceptive, it seemed.

I pretended to look for Briggy out in the lake, she was somewhere canoeing. Now the rain stopped. Mr Huggan: "What department are you in?"

I told him.

"What d'you actually do?"

"Write speeches, briefs."

"Do people do that sort of thing?" Beads of ice rattled between Huggan's teeth.

"He should have moved to Kingston—to be with me," Suzan came in and said.

"Then he'd be out of work," Mrs Huggan cried.

Suzan spoke only to her father next. "He could come and join our co-op; we're having a good time, some real discussions. We all get along well, like a family." The word "family" hung in the air.

"I wonder where the young people are heading nowadays," Bill Huggan said, also looking into the vastness of the lake. Mrs Huggan offered a wan smile. The grind of the power saw becoming a persistent whine. Suzan, well, it was hard to tell what was going through her mind now. That old man in Kingston again?

Briggy returned, rain-soaked as before, said a quick, chirpy hello to her father. Then she and Suzan started working in the kitchen. Mrs Huggan began assisting.

"When's Bob coming in?" Briggy asked, as if only now remembering her younger brother. Her father, as if obliged to answer: "He will come in late, after eleven."

"That late?"

Suzan: "He should phone, to let us know if he's really coming; it's been ages since I last saw him." Mrs Huggan made a chuffing noise. Then her husband, as if he was some distance away, said: "Montreal City Hall shouldn't make people work so late."

"It's the train. It takes a long time for the last train to get into the Laurentians," explained Briggy.

Steve entered, growling something to his parents, then went in and out of the kitchen. Suzan gave him a beer as he growled a thank-you and went back to continue with the saw. Cutlery, dishes, pots, pans, clattering. The lake lapped louder. Mr Huggan studied me from his easy chair: he often sat there, I figured. Mrs Huggan moved to the opposite side on the small settee, her fixed place.

The smell of food: Briggy said she had never felt so hungry. The ham, asparagus soaked in butter; the bread Mrs Huggan bought, now being sliced. Cold cuts, slivers of ham, salmon. Lettuce, cucumber, tomatoes in olive oil. Flowers handpicked, laid out: Suzan had gotten them, she said and looked at me, solicitous, wanting me to be at ease.

I said I was enjoying myself, and the food was really good. Slowly I sipped my glass of wine, remembering details of a long-concluded trip meant for Israel. But Ali had appeared speaking poetically to her, his rambling words about religious devotion; something I didn't want to hear. Strange I'd remember this, even as I'd write a ministerial briefing note. Was Suzan really in love with him? And she wanted him to come and live with her in Montreal, didn't she? But he wouldn't give up on Lebanon to come and wash dishes in Canada, he'd said.

Briggy next saying she loved sports, she was truly an outdoors type. Suzan muttering again about Kingston, while her mother chewed quickly, pulling at a piece of bread lodged between her teeth. "Very soon we'd start our own newspaper; at the co-op I mean," said Suzan. "We'd like the whole of Kingston to know what we're doing. We can't rely on the press releases used by the *Whig Standard.*"

"Or the *Queen's Journal,*" I quipped. My own days with the university rag: where I'd gotten to know Suzan one night at a party, and where she'd met this Greek who said to her: "Kissing you is like tasting fresh fruits in spring!" Suzan never seemed to have forgotten that line.

Just when I was thinking her mother wouldn't say a word, Mrs Huggan muttered: "Maybe you should do journalism, Suzan, at one of the community colleges."

"So you can tell your friends your daughter is doing something useful, Mom?" Suzan involuntarily raised her voice.

Briggy laughed, then said she preferred being in the lake—nowhere else. Her father kept looking around for his Scotch, even as he swallowed a sliver of salmon and nearly choked. "When's Bob coming in?" he asked again, and glanced at me—as if I would know.

"He should be here now; it's after eight," Steve said.

"It's close to nine," shrieked Briggy.

"Is it that late already?" Steve, speaking only for the second time.

"What's holding him up?" asked Mrs Huggan, wincing. "It'll soon be dark."

"You should phone Montreal," urged Bill Huggan, closing his eyes.

The clatter of cutlery next. Then Steve got up to return to his power saw. The lake lapping noisily because of a strong wind. Briggy chirped with black humour, "Maybe the train got derailed," and winked at me, fluttering her eyelashes. Mrs Huggan suddenly slumped backwards.

"Or," Suzan countered, "he has taken the bus. It's a longer ride." She too was becoming worried as she looked at her mother. I glanced from one to the other, her mother's colour darkening: it was funny, no one else was noticing this. Maybe the light was playing tricks on her face. I glanced at Suzan returning from the kitchen, putting things away noisily.

Briggy reappeared at intervals, looking intently at her parents, whose eyes were starting to close. The cottage air, lake, rain: all making for a soporific atmosphere. No sound of the power saw now, but an occasional crashing noise, branches pulled. Mrs Huggan fidgeted, hand reaching out for her drink, same as her husband did. Her half-opened eyes: that newspaper. "It'd be nice to see it get off its feet, Suzan," she said. "Montreal needs something like that too."

"It'll never happen in Montreal. It's too big a city. People are preoccupied with other things," Suzan offered, seriously.

"Yes, it could. Like the *Glebe Report*," I agreed, a community paper I had contributed to in Ottawa.

Suzan smiled, looking at me, then once more at her mother's crumpled, but equine face. The older woman brushed away an imaginary fly with an instinctive movement of her hand, then gave a nervous reaction as her jaw twitched. Suzan gripped my hand, nails almost digging in. Ali? Where was he now? Briggy mumbled something from somewhere about health; she was reading a really interesting new book on the subject. "You should read it too, Suzan," she called out. "What?" Suzan yelled back.

Briggy said, "Where will he sleep?" She meant me.

"Next to you, I guess." Suzan chirped. Then, "Phil will sleep in Bob's room."

Mrs Huggan opened her eyes. Raindrops' pitter-patter, and I looked at Mrs Huggan, then from the window turned to see the moon come out clearly, like a giant ball about to be lodged right in front of us, an angle of it reflected in the water, almost surreal-looking.

The sound of a car broke the silence. "It's Bob!" cried Mrs Huggan. "It's him!"

"What?" asked Mr Huggan, stirring.

Bob, tall, but hefty, every inch his eighteen years, entered with a huge unapologetic grin. He chuckled as Suzan hugged him, swinging against him as if at a tree. "Suzan!" he hollered. "It's so good to see

*46*

you!" Mr Huggan stirred once more: "Is that you, Bob? What kept you so long? We've been waiting up for you." And Mrs Huggan, "Have you had your supper yet? What kept you so long?" An unmistakably irascible tone.

"I was with friends," Bob lied, grinning. "I was getting this ride, too. I had to wait."

"Wait for what?" asked Mr Huggan.

"The ride, I just told you."

"What ride?

"Home. "

"To the cottage, Dad," chirped Briggy.

"You should've phoned," moaned Mrs Huggan.

Silence, as I looked at Mrs Huggan, wrinkles on her face cracking in the dim light. Bob, again chuckling, shaking my hand, then going to the kitchen and opening the refrigerator. "I guess I will eat something, though I'm not that hungry," he said.

"You must be," cried Mrs Huggan. "Now . . . what time is it? Eleven o'clock already!"

"I am not hungry. Besides I was with the guys, Mom."

"You must eat something!" his mother insisted.

Bob noisily pulled at the oven door, holding it ajar. There was the casserole inside, which Briggy said she'd made earlier. Mrs Huggan said, "Because you're working now, you think you can do as you like, Bob. You're still my baby!"

"I am a grown person, Mom!

"You're still my baby!"

"He is an adult, Mom," argued Suzan.

"You keep out of this!"

"I am just telling—"

"This is between Bob and me, you understand? Keep out!"

Suzan sulked.

"You don't know what's it like to raise him. You don't. Wait until you marry and have children of your own. Then you'll see what it's like!" Mrs Huggan sniffled tears. She looked at me and seemed a little embarrassed. Folds of skin, her wrinkles: like a gradual change-over. Mr Huggan looked at her fixedly, as if he too saw what I saw. Mrs Huggan continued, "You're in Kingston, what do you know? What d'you think you're doing with your life. All of you!" She started sobbing.

Mr Huggan raised himself on his haunches, face glowing in the dim light. Mrs Huggan turned from her husband to Bob again. "You should have phoned!"

"I did, Mom!"

Mrs Huggan: "Just because they think they've grown, they're no longer your children!" She looked unforgivingly at Suzan, before shifting her gaze to me once more, as if I was the one leading Suzan astray. Unless she figured I could "save" Suzan.

Something kept me glued to Mrs Huggan: her face, eyes smaller as they now seemed. I turned, looking at Suzan, for the first time noting the resemblance between mother and daughter. Her father jolted back to his seat, as if pulled back. Then he closed his eyes, though his right hand mechanically reached out for a drink: another Scotch.

"Oh Mom," laughed Bob, eating something stringy, pasta, moaning in mock lamentation.

"You're all ungrateful!" hissed Mrs Huggan.

"Knock it off, Mom," Bob answered. "You will only harm yourself, with your weak heart." All eyes widened. Weak heart?

Suzan stiffened, as I looked from her to her mother, then at Bob. Mrs Huggan opened and closed her eyes. And I knew then that Suzan didn't know her mother had a weak heart. Now she was feeling twinges of remorse; the past with her mother, and now, this.

Mrs Huggan sunk back into her chair. Bill Huggan kept reaching out for his drink. "Mom, I didn't know you had a weak heart," said Suzan. "I won't die just yet, if that's what you're thinking," came a curt reply.

"Of course not, Mom."

Bob: "Mom's been seeing a doctor regularly for the past six months.

"Why didn't you tell me before?" Suzan scolded.

Bob shrugged.

"Mom, you should have told me also," insisted Suzan.

"What do you care?" Mrs Huggan brutally said. "You and your co-op. Would you have time for me?"

"Of course, Mom!" Suzan's eyes blazed.

Briggy held up her health book. "Well, it may not be as bad as all that. Mom'll be okay before long," she said.

"She will?" asked Steve, making himself known.

It was as if I wasn't there with them any longer, the way the conversation flowed. From time to time Suzan looked in my direction, as I yawned. She too yawned. Bob got up and went to the kitchen. At this point Mrs Huggan fell forward, gasped, let out a heavy moan.

I looked at her, transfixed. Suzan frowned, then: "Dad!"

Bill Huggan opened his eyes and stared at everyone, unpleasantly awakened from a pleasant dream. "Mom's having a heart attack!" cried Suzan.

Bob sprang up, peering at his mother, then with surprising calm, he said: "She's never looked like this before, ashen."

"Get her pills," said Mr Huggan.

"Her pills!" yelled Suzan, to Briggy and me, as if I knew where the pills were.

Slumped backward now, Mrs Huggan moaned again, her hands at her throat, then at her chest, apparently unable to breathe. "Where are the pills?" cried Bob, looking stupefied.

"Briggy, where are they?" Suzan yelled.

Briggy, still clutching her health book, looked calm. She even glanced at me, as if about to smile, then didn't. Bob rushed into the bedroom, came out empty handed, rushed in again, with Briggy behind him this time. Steve made a move also, though he was closer to the door, about to slither out, back to his power saw.

"Christ," let out Suzan's father, "somebody should know where she keeps her pills. I hope she doesn't have one of her serious attacks now."

"We should call an ambulance," I offered. But I was looked at disdainfully.

Mr Huggan: "She'll be okay. It has happened before. Once she gets her pills, she'll be okay."

"You sure, Dad?" Suzan asked.

"Eh?" he barked,

"Will she be okay?"

"For Chrissake, yes. What am I—a doctor?"

Mrs Huggan's mouth closed, face more ashen, upper lip twitching. Eyelids aflutter.

"She looks terrible, Dad," said Briggy. "Maybe this is for real."

"It's always been for real, for Christ's sake!" he snapped.

"I will get the truck started," said Steve, moving closer to the door.

"What for?" shouted Mr Huggan.

"To take her out."

"Where?" Huggan rasped.

Mrs Huggan opened her eyes and smiled weakly, one hand reaching out, clawing the air: reaching out for Bob maybe, as she moaned again. Then she gasped once more. "Have . . . have you . . . eaten, son?"

Bob nodded.

"You're still . . . my baby, you know. You're all I have."

"Mom, you have us, what about us?" said Briggy.

Mrs Huggan's eyes swivelled, and she also glanced at Suzan and repeated: "You're all I have left."

I wasn't sure if she was speaking to me as well, as I watched her fixedly, in an awkward moment. "We must get her to the truck," said Steve, stiff as a pole.

"What for?" repeated Huggan.

"I will start the truck," Steve said, ignoring his father.

Suzan kept feeling helpless, her hand tightening in mine, and she felt reassured because I was close to her; maybe for the first time in years, something unimaginable or unpredictable was happening with us now.

"She'll be okay before long, once she swallows those pills," said Bill Huggan, uncorking the bottle which Briggy handed him.

Mrs Huggan slowly took a couple of pills into her mouth, like a stork swallowing fish.

"I think she'll be sick all weekend, Dad," Bob said, looking ashen himself. He seemed contrite also, figuring her attack was due to his coming home late.

"No . . . maybe not," said the older man, looking around for his glass of Scotch and bringing it to his lips.

Just then Briggy hollered, "Christ, Dad, Mom's been drinking. She's not supposed to drink and take those pills!"

"What?" asked Huggan.

"The pills! I tell you, she's not supposed to!"

Suzan felt numb, her hand still in mine.

But Huggan muttered disconsolately, "She's done it before."

"Christ, she will die!" yelled Briggy.

Steve stood at the door and calmly said, "I am ready."

Everyone looked at him, and Huggan—as if he knew he didn't have a choice any longer—shrugged, while Bob, Steve, and Briggy began pulling their mother up. Suzan's hand was still in mine; and the thought occurred to me that Mrs Huggan's illness might be due to something psychological.

Suzan started crying; Mrs Huggan's face seemed yellow, then green in the dim light. The lake lapping harder as the moon seemed to have come closer. "I am sorry, Mom. Gosh, I am so sorry," cried Suzan, as they began lifting Mrs Huggan to the door. Bill Huggan was close to me, on one side, and Bob and Steve were on the other.

Huggan muttered, almost inaudibly to me: "What did you say you do in the government?" He didn't wait for me to answer. "To think it should happen this weekend." He kept looking at me. "Did you say you're Jewish?"

Suzan, close by now, merely muttered something about the old man in Kingston who lived alone on Bagot Street, whose life was slowly coming to an end. Mrs Huggan grimaced, as I focused on the moon coming closer. Yes, the same as I'd seen once in the Middle East. But never in Ottawa. Just then Mrs Huggan's eyes opened widely and fell on Suzan.

Then her eyes closed again.

Suzan turned and looked at me: her own eyes in a sustained glow, thinking perhaps of a faraway place we might have traveled to; and still wanted to go to again before it was too late. The lake's quiet rhythm all its own, as I felt swept away by it, with the moon again coming low, and I unconsciously was reaching out to touch it. "We would be alone," I heard Suzan mutter.

# Departure

My turn, and the Immigration Officer looked at me, askance. "This letter," he began.

I waited, anxious. I was before Mr Horsman himself, the feared, the dreaded one.

He kept looking at me.

I managed a smile; maybe I was trying to be beguiling. The letter said I should not have come here, to Canada. Did it really?

Oh?

He scoffed, as the letter wavered in his hand. My heart started beating faster. Then, Why not?—I wanted to say to him, but couldn't. My tongue was cleaved to the roof of my mouth.

He was thinking, and I could see it in his face, eyes, as my anxiety grew by leaps and bounds. Mr Horsman's reputation was well known: he'd sign a document that would easily send you out of Canada. Immediate deportation! Such power he had; his authority was unquestionable. Yes, all done with one stroke of the pen. And who hadn't heard of him?

Mr Horsman smiled, maybe thinking of where I'd come from, my origins: memories intact in me, my consciousness; and he had an inkling of it all. Imagine that. Oddly, I also felt him going back with me there, as perhaps I wanted him to: he actually in the plane with me, in our strange yet eloquent silence. A long journey, meshing our thoughts.

He looked at me from across his large mahogany desk.

I blinked.

Then deliberately he leant towards the documents before him, my papers, and with a large-nibbed pen he began writing. Ink flowing, like blood. Again he stared at me from behind large, horn-rimmed glasses. "Do you like Canada?" he asked, unbending.

"Eh?"

"Canada?"

"Oh, er, yes." My spirit, body, still frozen as more fear entered me; this shortish, bald man in his late fifties, dignified-looking. Again I began seeing him sending fear into others, those who'd been here before me: all summoned to report to his office. They'd been living illegally in Canada. Somehow they'd entered the country and remained. Some were students with visas that weren't valid. Now they'd be sent out of Canada with one stroke of Mr Horsman's pen!

Why just then I didn't believe what I'd heard before about Mr Horsman. Like an awakening, a new spirit or thought in me, throbbing. Yet I remained mum.

He took his time inhaling, and then his face was covered by a beatific, flitting smile, transforming him. "You will visit places?" he asked.

Was he tempting, baiting me?

"Well, er . . . yes," I managed.

"What province?"

"Province?"

"Towns, cities, won't you like to visit each one?" He laughed.

I also laughed, instinctively .

His eyes strange-looking, shimmering.

"To experience all the rivers, lakes, the thousands in Canada?"

"Yes," I said, hurriedly.

*54*

"To take in every image of the new land, the full terrain, all of Canada."

What was he saying?

"The flora, true northern tundra."

I smiled.

"Go far up north, the northwest and Nunavut, to see the caribou, reindeer, all in their natural setting."

"Maybe."

He kept looking at me, with the same beatific smile.

The wolf, bear, moose . . . ? He held up his pen. The hard nib. Blood, ink; and the full landscape, amidst the memory of another place, where I'd come from. Now it was only Canada where I wanted to belong, had thought much about, nowhere else. No other country, not America, Australia, or places in Europe, Latin America.

In Canada, only.

Mr Horsman kept smiling. An inkling of something in me, him. All places, territories, with us, in us.

I kept a tight look in my eyes: a matter of will. Yes, the feared, dreaded Mr Horsman, smiling. But no more?

He grimaced next. And a scowl sent all my hopes dashing. What real surprises were ahead? Wait until I tell the others.

Mr Horsman held up his pen again.

Now.

"You must visit places," he added. And he wasn't just playing a game with me. Then I thought I heard him say next: "Please, we want you; all of Canada wants you."

I wasn't believing my ears. Again I instinctively laughed.

He too laughed, like an echo.

This moment, the document—my complete file before him—which he must have contemplated for hours, I figured, I wanted to believe. My case was special. Yes, he would sign now, affix his signature, which meant I could stay in Canada as long as I wanted. I'd be free to do as I wanted. "Go on," I said, mutely. Suddenly I didn't want to be a Canadian, because I figured I would have to remain here forever; I would always be tagged a *Canadian*; and I wouldn't belong to any other place, but here. Ah, what is a Canadian?

The pen hovering.

Why was I here? I wanted to run out of his office, and from my fear, something I'd imagined all along. Yet the fear was disappearing; and what I'd imagined about Mr Horsman was also disappearing.

Now every image, grass, leaf, all the flora and fauna of the Canadian landscape, seemed to be part of my own, my very own, if I became a Canadian. And Mr Horsman was bent on indeed turning me into one. With one stroke of the pen. No! The responsibility was too much.

"Wait," I said, lifting a hand.

"What?" He seemed alarmed.

"I do not want to stay here."

"I thought you . . . did!"

"Not any longer, Mr Horsman."

"There must be a reason for your refusal." He became genuinely disappointed. Aghast even. And I began to see him differently, he who had intimidated so many others, feared by all. Yes, Mr Horsman, the Immigration Officer . . . once he pulled out your file, it meant the end of your stay here despite claiming to be a refugee, or foreign student.

"Yes, there is," I said, answering him, trying to appear calm.

"Is that . . . it?" He looked at me, still dumbfounded.

"Must I tell you? Must I?" I was searching for words, thinking of what to say, precisely; and maybe I sneered a little.

"Yes?" he encouraged.

"Well . . . I won't."

He waited, not sure what to make of me; yet he held up his pen. "Unless you don't want to live in Canada, you want to go somewhere else. To America, or Europe . . . ?" He paused, reflecting.

"Asia. Africa, the Middle East?" he tried next, with his hard glare. "Everywhere, but Canada, right?"

"Right."

He burst out laughing, his body seeming smaller, his head more bald, gums wide and pinkish, and he looked odd, comical even.

Suddenly I felt the world was mine; I could go wherever I wanted, couldn't I?

Anywhere.

He lowered his head, and it was as if the pen was no more in his hand; it had dropped, the ink oozing, forming a messy blob. Then the pen was empty, like blood in a person running dry. And he was now waiting for me to wave, with a sense of victory.

I remained looking at the pen.

The papers on the desk before him, the document waiting for his signature of approval, with the stamp of Canada on it, the maple leaf no less.

Slowly I began gathering the letters, pieces of papers; and I stretched out a hand and mechanically held his across the mahagony desk, and I was guiding him, telling him to sign.

Yes, sign, there!

He did.

And he seemed relieved, because the burden he carried all along was too much. And he wanted me gone from his office; really gone.

But I remained with him, and quietly, mutely, asked him about all the others he'd sent back to their far-off lands, all the distant places: out of Canada.

Yes, tell me everything, Mr Horsman. Tell me of the pain you caused. Families not ever being united. Children crying, because they were unable to see one or more of their parents for months, years. Such anguish. Yes, do not leave out anything.

Slowly he began talking, about the faces he remembered. They could have all become Canadians, he admitted; people who could've made their mark on this soil, on this vast land.

"Tell me more, Mr Horsman."

"More?"

"Please, don't stop now."

"There's not more to tell."

"Keep nothing from me."

"I am . . . not. How dare you?"

"You mustn't deny it," I scoffed.

He seemed humble, almost defeated. And indeed I wanted him to admit everything: to experience the guilt of all his past actions. Yes, all those deported, sent back there: to South and Central America, Asia, the Caribbean; the empty, drought-stricken plains of Africa; the barren soil of vagrant parts of Europe, all war-torn. Yes, people still in the slums of unnamed cities, countries: who all had dreamt of becoming Canadian. But no more.

No more?

He looked me in the eyes.

I stared back at him.

And that beatific expression again, as if all was forgiven.

I smiled vaguely.

The pen in his hand, in this building in a city that could be Toronto, Ottawa, Thunder Bay, Saskatoon, or Winnipeg. A large place anyhow, right here in Canada. He started writing. An apology?

*Please.*

And I began imagining moving across Canada, going from the Atlantic to all of Quebec, Ontario, across the Prairies, to Alberta, and next to the Rocky Mountains; going farther west, and looking back over the distances I'd travelled.

And more. "Much more," I shouted.

The mountains, echoing the words to me. "Much more," to all the rivers and lakes. "Much more . . . more!" I heard myself cry out. And Mr Horsman was hearing these words, like a halloo; voices resounding also in a cave or memory-source, distant yet close up.

I held my fingers to my ears, suddenly wishing the noise to stop; and maybe I was on my own last journey, and my own voice was crying out in Canada, where I was not the one and true Canadian I'd imagined myself to be.

I looked at the apology written: clear and crisp, the one word. "Sorry."

And it seemed I was meeting him for the first time, and all the others were with me, those from foreign lands, muttering voicelessly, saying he was a stalwart in a way: he who had inspired such fear all along because he was a Canadian.

Ah, I was now one like him: I was his equal.

And we were looking at the world together, as one.

# Going to Guyana

Why I wanted miracles to happen as I boarded the Guyana Airways jet at the Miami International Airport in steamy, swirling heat, I didn't know. A sense of parody or pantomime mixed with a vague feeling of loyalty to a mud-brown, alluvium-and-silt-clogged land kept me sitting up straight as the plane jolted and accelerated along the driveway, then finally took off.

I'd been living in Canada much too long, and now I felt compelled to return. Chris (short for Krishna) everyone called me, a name too familiar, devoid of resonance; and I'd put off returning until now, wrestling with an awkward but prolonged alienation, in the country; as with women, in infatuation or love. Don't get me wrong, I kept on socializing. "You could get any girl you want," said French-Canadian Nicole, my current date. "Just put on a navy blue blazer, and smile." But Nicole also hinted that I sometimes made her depressed because of an unexpected absentmindedness. Why wasn't I given to dancing all night, as she wanted? Once I caught her studying my shoes, and she said she could tell a lot about a man by his footwear. She could? Allusion to penile prowess? I told her I'd often walked barefoot for long hours as a child on my way to school in a foreign land, the dreary tropical heat bearing down on me, which I could never forget. Ah, I wasn't going to deny my origin.

Now in midair, floating in space with all worlds turning, anxiety rising because of what was ahead, or what not to expect. A tallish, slender-looking stewardess in mauve, charcoal-hued suit, kept walking gracefully along the aisle, as I looked at her; and I kept thinking of having travelled often in Canada, criss-crossing a vast land because of my work on behalf of the Canadian government, which was how I'd met Nicole. I'd immediately liked her ease, a touch of Mohawk in her too, casually mentioned when we were together one night, as she'd muttered that I didn't look "Asian."

The plane humming, and I kept looking outside into the vagueness of clouds, oddly longing for ancestry.

"So why are you going back there after all these years?" the lanky hostess in mauve asked me in a surprising moment.

I shrugged.

Clouds moving mirage-like, with passengers getting up, forming a constant stream along the aisle where an odd assortment of baggage, parcels, material was stuffed in every corner of the plane it seemed: in every jot of space between their legs, the sides. A growing listlessness and yet frenzy in me amidst the plane's drone, with everyone wanting to get there quickly.

Strangely now I felt no strong obligation to return, the plane seeming at a standstill, as if somewhere amongst thick trees, forests, my mind in a lull. Then she came again, the lanky hostess. Who was she? I tried to pigeon-hole her by race, origin, the more aloof she looked and the higher we climbed . . . and drew closer to the tropics. Fragments of time and place: canefields, trade wind wafting. The other stewardesses walked by, but it was Arabella—the lanky one—I kept looking at even during the sudden turbulence: the plane pitching, the passengers restless. A Chinese man, surprisingly tall, stretched out his arms windmill-fashion unwittingly hitting out. An African, an immediate victim, grimaced.

A scuffle in midair, with rebukes, name-calling, of a distinct racial cast.

"Is wha' happen to you, man?" cried a midair combatant. "You not see you hittin me?"

A screeching response from the other: "Man, you talkin' like you still back there?"

Snickers, then laughter as the parody was acted out among the passengers. Arabella pursed her lips, and everyone expected her to mediate. "Let them fight," she calmly said.

The African sucked his teeth with a sharply hissing noise. The Chinese yelled a further rebuke, his eyes a full glare. An obay mulatto woman who'd boarded the plane from New York City let out her own flurry of words. Laughter echoed down her section of the aisle, mainly from an older man whose jaws moved up and down like a strange contraption. "You all lookout wid this Guyana plane," he said. "Someone goin' to take it over in midair cause the government not able to pay the rent. Guyana now blasted bankrupt!"

Arabella yawned, appearing as if she'd been through this before, then murmured: "No one's going to take over this plane." Her fixed sultriness reigned. "The Captain tell you to say that, girl?" came a retort from another passenger.

"No Captain goin' tell her to say that," someone else hissed. "Women not stupid nowadays."

Arabella kept up a determinedly aloof air.

"How d'you know?" snapped another.

After a short silence, someone said we'd soon be flying over Havana, which caused a screech: "We're no longer communists cause socialism's done for." Only Arabella didn't seem amused. The captain's voice on the intercom came to indicate our flying time, like destiny itself.

Arabella again passed by the aisle and looked at me intently, as someone else added: "A plane can withstand all kinds o' pressure, even if it's a blasted Cuban communist plane."

"Yes," came a quick answer. Then collective laughter followed, echoing everywhere.

*

The entire six-hour flight was now becoming an eternity, as I kept conjuring up an ocean, green grass, all of the "tropical paradise" I was returning to: a place close to Venezuela; and thoughts of Georgetown, the capital, being lashed by tidal waves despite the seawall, mangrove and courida . . . threatening the entire coastland. My father's own backlands imprinted in me: he still there, hoary headed, herons picking at his thin-bodied cattle on muddy coastal ground in the Canje district. Scooping up cow's urine from a fissure in the ground to salve his thirst in the wilderness of the place.

One passenger, then another, got up as if searching for an exit. A voice close to me said: "Maybe we'll never land there." My tongue's own clacking sensation, dry-mouthed. Then a louder voice called: "Guyana not so green anymore."

"God, you don't have to bad-talk we country. We born there," came a high-spirited rejoinder. Arabella seemed not so aloof any-more, now that we were closer to "home."

The trade wind whirling against coconut trees leaning like tall old men against zinc-roofed houses. Night's onslaught of rain causing all to sway and bend, the thunder-crack of an entire forest overwhelming in the plane's sudden dive and inevitable crash. A cry escaped my lips: I'd been sleeping and was having a nightmare.

The man next to me nudged me fully awake. Further images, the black-watered creek in the Canje with dog fish or perai. Clusters of water hyacinths, algae, amidst flowers bursting out in effulgent sun-light everywhere.

"Tired?" came a voice, Arabella bringing me back to the present, hips barely pressing against my shoulder. "Maybe you're not so eager to return." A rasp in her voice, discomfiture. Banana leaves, the creek's shimmering haze; and she smiled, and maybe to her time did not matter anymore.

"Things have changed," she said.

"Are you telling me?"

Syllables rounded out, the dialect of silence echoing nostalgia's powerful grip on me . . . as we drew closer to Guyana with further tremors and impulses of home. Arabella quivering, I sensed. "Have you ever thought of leaving yourself?" I asked.

"Never." Her lips tightened.

"Why not?"

She became quietly wistful. "I come and go all the time. You and your kind, also come an' go." Her hips wilfully swayed, carrying all of the aisle with her.

I rubbed my eyes. A few passengers rousing from their own short naps made instant catcalls, hissing at her. Did they? The captain's voice again, announcing that before long we'd be in Guyana. A ritual excitement in the cabin. The next moment I was the captain himself, steering this large insect of a plane, losing altitude. Someone laughed in anticipation, then the captain's monotone voice once more: "I'm afraid, ladies and gentlemen, we can't land there just yet."

"Why not?" cried a hundred voices all at once.

The captain's professional drone: "There are no lights at the Guyana airport."

"No lights?" a tight gasp, hiss.

"Electricity breakdown, you see," said too matter-of-factly.

I looked out in the mirage and aura of hinterland, jungle looming up, thinking of Timehri Airport and primitive paintings reminiscent of aboriginal wall art. The captain apologizing—the plane would now go to the neighbouring airport, in Surinam.

Someone started hiccoughing. Arabella—as if she expected this—wagged a finger at him. Outside, the darkness, rock paintings: figures of ancient Caribs, Arawaks darting about in impenetrably bunched forest. The hiccoughing got louder. Night's unwelcoming: the plane turning around, throbbing. . .going away from Timehri.

I rubbed my eyes in the changing light: reality. . . Canada, North America, all far away as if in a different time, a different planet or galaxy.

*

Four o'clock in the morning: our weird fate to be here at this time, as the mood changed from dull excitement to listlessness, then desperation. Sounds from another scuffle: now an East Indian, very thin, pointing a finger and saying: "It's your kind, you are to blame. The politicians of your race—that's why we're here." Words charged with an overwhelming sense of exile, or outraged ethnicity: this amidst more vegetation in a genuine chiaroscuro world, then darkness, intermittent light. The obay woman shrieking an accusation about corrupt politics in the Third World. Another, less loud: "All I'm concerned about is getting home safely. I fear for my safety in this Godforsaken place. I fear every blasted thing now: snake, tarantula, scorpion. God, I want to get back to America!"

Another, behind me, cried, "Is we bad luck to arrive here"—as if thrust into a hollow vortex of rage. "God," the wrinkled East Indian man's turn, again, "my family would be waiting for me at the airport all night long. I last saw them ten years ago. Now I am here, in another country. What for?" He burst out laughing crazily, adding, "Next time I'm travelling Air Canada."

"Not Pan Am?" someone jeered from the opposite end of the plane.

When suddenly the ground heaved, I saw Arabella coming out of the captain's cabin, her hair slightly tousled. Maybe now she'd tell us if indeed there was a blackout at Timehri: so strange in this age of universal electrification; or if there was a coup taking place in Guyana.

Coup?

Guns firing, staccato coughs of bullets; cinematic image after image, recurring, rearranging. Arabella defying my suspicions because she really knew, and the captain also knew. The motley group of passengers, dumbfounded, also knew, but me. The East Indian man wailed, "I shoulda never been born in such a place as—"

But another rejoined, "Where you want to be born then, in England?"

"Na, America," came a sharp-tongued reply.

Why not Canada? I turned, intent on looking at the last speaker. But Arabella again drew closer, face florid, perhaps now defying me to ask about Guyana. My quick recollection or consciousness: history, a place still known as paradise or a long-lost El Dorado as I'd often told French-Canadian Nicole; and Sir Walter Raleigh gallantly throwing his coat across a ditch for the Queen to step out on. . . followed by a vision of the dreaded Tower of London.

Arabella laughed as someone else hissed: "Yes, is America we'll end up in anyway."

"Not Canada—where everyone's immigrating to nowadays?"

"It too damn cold there," drummed another.

"Too far from the blasted equator?"

We quickly landed in the steamy, sultry Surinam heat where soldiers conspicuously milled about in heavy-booted fashion.

Arabella standing next to a determined chocolaty-looking first officer, the tallest man I ever saw, with voices hissing all around, haranguing about America, Canada. Next came a ghettoblaster's celebration or invasion, reggae sounds amid Dutch gibberish.

Arabella, as I watched her, again muttered to the pilot who was leaning closer to her, as if about to start nibbling her ear, all in the familiarity of further colloquialism. Someone else, one of the combatants—the Chinese—hovering in the darkness let out: "We could collectively change things around here. Bring in big investment from Hong Kong, Japan, all of Southeast Asia."

"It'd be exploitation whichever way you think about it," a bespectacled woman—an intellectual or zealot—answered.

"Look at America, it built on exploitation," the Chinese man retorted.

"The exploitation of blacks!" the obay one caterwauled.

The first officer now tried speaking to the passengers one by one, exhorting them to be patient: the frailty, predictability all around, resolutely muttering that before long we'd arrive at our destination. And he yet again blamed the ubiquitous blackout.

Laughter.

Arabella's breast rose, and so different she appeared now, troubled-looking. Amidst the ghettoblaster's loud peal, like derangement, with Bob Marley's "Burning Spear," she again drew closer to me in perplexing light and darkness at this hour. "You know," she said, "I'd once thought of emigrating. But I hate filling out all those damn forms. Those awful questions they ask, they want to know everything about you."

She had been leaving all the time, for places in Arabia, the Far East, all she had read about and imagined.

"I wanted to leave Guyana badly. But then I always think about Albouystown, that alley where I came from."

I listened with growing fascination and curiosity; she was becoming increasingly nostalgic. "My family's still there." The intensity on her face, eyes quivering. Why then did I imagine her a model in Paris, London, New York: a professional photographer on Fifth Avenue taking shots of her at different angles, all her natural flair?

"I could never really leave," she grated.

But we were ready to leave Surinam now, finally heading home for Guyana.

*

Timehri, our rushing up to it in the cabin's excitement as everyone got jolted into full consciousness. Soon there would be the loud greetings of relatives, friends. Arabella's head tilted back, she laughed. The trade wind and the ghettoblaster's reggae still in my ears, the line to the customs officials quickly becoming a crowd, a scrimmage, with more soldiers milling about. One thin, gangly youth let out, "Is where all-you come from?"

"America, where else?" came a strident reply.

Another grunted his impatience because he couldn't find his suitcase, blaming the inept customs staff, then sneered, "Gosh, they're yet to become efficient here."

Someone else added, "You'd think you're back in the dark ages," and strangely guffawed.

Arabella beckoned to me: she knew a way through customs, and the fastest taxi to Georgetown. Soon we were hurtling along on a tortuous road—leaving me breathless and yet staring at her lovely face as she shrieked with laughter. "Where are we going next?" the driver asked, the humid air reeking of burnt tire, with houses on stilts crashing down on us on all sides. Came Arabella's instinctive answer: "Albouystown." Not Jonestown?

Lips quivering, as if with religious tremor. The taxi veering, screeching to a halt next to a busy alleyway. Arabella said, "I want to show them I have a friend come from America." She meant me.

"Show them?"

"Yes." She smiled.

"I am from Canada."

But she was already encouraging that I take good note that there were no large houses here, as we stepped gingerly on mud-caked ground. She confidently led me through a maze of small huts and houses amidst ancient smells of paraffin, salted cod, rotten potatoes. What would French-Canadian Nicole now think of my being here? A dozen heads peeping out at once, gleeful children's faces; Arabella waving to them, their contrasting expressions, teeth jutting out whitely against black lips. The eyes almost incandescent, asking: Who is he?

An older woman with a basket of fruit on her head—colourful mango, papaw, pineapple, banana—sauntered by, pointing, asking who I was, or wasn't. Arabella's eyes flickered as we stood before a corrugated-looking hovel.

Sinewy, webbed faces, arms, dozens of them, were now all around Arabella, as if she'd been away for years. Faces, mouths, the old and young alike, all welcoming her. "I bring home a friend, Ma," she said to the oldest woman around.

I inhaled more of the mixture of iodine, cough syrup, stale food, old clothes, overripe banana. Other zinc-topped houses around, in a sudden shimmering brilliance everywhere.

Arabella said, "He come from America, but I can show him we're all the same," and emitted a throaty laugh as she glanced fully at me. "Look at he good," she added.

Eyes searching me in unabashed curiosity, then they started laughing. Nicole, do you hear? Do I still look "Asian"? Arabella: "See, America's made no change in him all these years."

Hands pawing me, all of Guyana pressing closer to me. An old man, small-headed, looked at me in a grandfatherly way, and other old women and men, webby hands, rheumy eyed, bending forward to look closely at me. Arabella started calling out their names one by one, as a child close to me chanted: "America-America," pink tongue sticking out. The old woman droning like a bee, her words yet audible: "So you're really from 'merica?"

"It mek no difference," someone else cackled.

Arabella took my hand, and it dawned on me that in North America maybe nothing was ever real. But here, in this Albouystown alley with all the faces still looking at me, would they ask me about skyscrapers, cars, videos, TV's, fridges, computers, washing machines? Bare gums, chapped lips, still asking.

Arabella's face sculpted with intensity, as another muttered about Africa: there where Arabella might have been a princess. Ah, her actually being on the cover of *Vogue*. I imagined a photographer's indulgence or extravagance.

I was hungry, and before long on the table was put salted cod reeking in coconut oil. Tomatoes, plantains, cassava, other vegetables such as okra. They watched as I ate, quickly. A fleck of oil dripping from a side of Arabella's mouth, a pink tomato skin clinging to her lower lip.

I wiped my lips.

The children tittering.

I sucked at a bone next, holding it between my teeth.

"Eat good," the old woman urged.

"Maybe you will never go back to 'merica," another muttered. Arabella, I kept imagining, in a specially made diaphanous gown or evening dress, Manhattan's best, stunningly displayed on her. The designers, journalists, purchasers, buyers, admiring her elegance. Was she truly a long-lost African princess?

Outside, rain started pouring, water kicking up from the ground;

Arabella reassuring me that soon the sun would be out again, always the sense of changing tropical weather.

She quivered next, "You must leave here, though."

Lightning flashed, as Arabella laughed, inquiring about ice and snow in the same breath.

My temperate self, I reminded her, muttering about readjustment, while imagining beech, pine, spruce, as much as I was among taller trees in the greenhearted forest not far from us.

Impulsively I said, "Why not come with me to Canada?"

"Too cold there."

"I've survived."

"Don't tempt me." Still long gowned, diaphanous, I imagined her to be. "I belong here."

"There too."

She laughed.

"You know it." Why I said that, I didn't know; yet I detected her quickening heartbeat. Further tremors of day and night as the rain stopped. My further imagining: as we walked hand in hand, she still the center of attention and being interviewed on radio, TV. All of America, Europe, Africa, Asia: watch her good.

"No," she repeated, she wanted none of that, bracing herself against my invitation, new impulses.

The relatives encouraging her, urging: "Arabella, go with him. Have no fear."

Now I started fighting to come to grips with myself: with my ties of place, and my father not far away in the Canje, close to where thick vegetation floated down the narrow, sinuous creek. A bloated dead cow moving along with a brightly yellow kiskadee or heron perched on its back. Rich molasses smell in the air not far from a large cane factory. Next, a silk cotton tree swishing, long-memoried: associated with Dutch lore.

. . .Travelling farther down the Canje—Arabella and I—going to a place called Magdalenenburg where the first slave rebellion had occurred. More thick vegetation, roots of strange trees on continually

buttressed soil. A mandrake sky overhead, then becoming dark,
* blackened. A howler monkey's strange bark, presaging more torren-
tial rain.

Arabella clung to me. "We must leave at once." She breathed
harder.

Her relatives grinning as if they knew something about her I didn't.
Who really was Arabella? Nicole also asking; all of Canada, America, asking. My father now greeting us, and also asking. The place
called Magdalenenburg, and the early slaves also asking. Did they
recognize her? Did they? A really lost West African princess as she
was?

*

We started meeting again the other passengers from the plane at this
unpredictable time on the coastland; their recognizing Arabella,
never me. And it wasn't her fault that the country was like this, they
said. "We should never have come back here," the obay woman
hurled.

To Arabella I whispered, "I will remain here with you."

"Will you?"

Then we heard: "A coup has just taken place. The new government's decided to ban all flights out of the country."

This repeated in a singsong fashion on the radio, without malice or
hate, only with a surprising nonchalance or indifference.

Arabella shrugged. And immediately I imagined the two midair
combatants, the plane wobbling, with Arabella still close to me. Water swirling, leviathans crashing or tumbling in my sleep maybe.
Once more soldiers moving about because we were indeed in a state
of siege.

Instinctively I looked up, seeing another plane high above. Who
did it belong to?

Arabella also looking up. Some of the other passengers with us
pointing at it. Air Canada? Were they coming to help me escape from
the real danger they figured I was in because of the coup?

Ah, Nicole, she'd engineered it, hadn't she? She who (as she'd told me) was sometimes friendly with a high-ranking cabinet minister in Ottawa—maybe the Minister of Defence. And I was a Canadian government official, didn't you know? All possibilities about rescuing me because of the growing turmoil all around.

Arabella put a hand to her eyes, squinting. Slave drums beating, the silk cotton tree swishing funereally. My feet firmly planted on hard ground.

The others around Arabella, moving closer to her.

Nicole laughing, I suddenly heard, then muttering, "We heard about it—the coup." She did? Nicole admonishing me next: "See, I told you to wear a dark blazer and smile a lot"—her unfailing sense of humour. Did I still look "Asian"?

And Arabella, I kept looking around for her in the excitement because of the widening coup, she standing next to the old woman, her mother. They were both waving to me.

I also started waving and yet nodding to my hoary-headed father.

"Goodbye," I cried to him, one final time.

The intense heat of the tropics everywhere—. And Arabella was still looking at me from *Vogue*, or some other Paris or New York magazine. The obay one sitting next to me on the plane now, getting a ride back to New York, she said, adding with irony: "Young man, you belong with them; not up here where there are no combatants."

"None whatsoever," she added after a while.

In her laughter I heard Arabella's voice, and instinctively waved to them below, one more time, not believing it was my final parting: my disappearing act. Arabella waving back from below, with her entire family, it seemed. Waves beating in memory and consciousness, like the self disappearing across climates, against an assault, gunfire indeed in the strangest of acts.

Nicole instinctively moved closer to me; and then quietly started talking about being in love akin to being in a wilderness: she who wanted affection, not just passion, she said, in the breathtaking space of our going to a new place called home.

# Jet Lag

Canada has as many faces as a Buddhist deity.
GEORGE WOODCOCK

A place I had never visited before, and I was finally going there, to India: where over nine hundred million people lived. Where else? Let me admit, I'd been mistaken for an Indian. Mistaken?

I looked Indian, my features, even carriage and speech intonation; but I was born elsewhere: in South America, the Caribbean portion; and something about my wanting to be unique persisted.

Ancestry in me nevertheless, my unerring sense of it, and Mahatma Gandhi, Jawaharlal Nehru, other stalwarts who'd fought for independence during the days of the Raj, fired my imagination. I also recalled as a child hearing about India's independence celebrated with fanfare, the Indian flag waved by elders in South America, voices rising: "Jai Hind!" In my teenage years I'd read the great Bengali poet Rabindranath Tagore: his *Gitanjali* especially, famous for its lyricism and spiritualism, a copy of which a few of the diehard villagers walked around with and quoted verses from. I also lipped some of the words with deference (if not reverence).

Other Indian writers, thinkers too, I'd dwelled on; and then the reli-

73

gious texts, the Vedas, and reflecting on the great sages of the land of my forebears. Yet I figured I wasn't Indian; and maybe Canada had done this to me, made me think I was different. Indeed, the past was the past, done with.

In Canada where I lived, the heroes were the Founding Fathers, all with a vague sense of the Native Great Spirit. And as a Canadian I coped with harsh winter, ice and snow for eight months of the year, with none of the ease or languor of the tropics in me; though in odd moments of nostalgia dreams, images reappeared.

And now the sense of India's history and myth, like a throwback in time, all in the longing for roots. Rudyard Kipling's Mowgli too, I conjured up, associated with journey and the changing self. Uncertainties always surfacing . . . and would now be resolved in my going to India.

In preparation for the visit, I secured translations of the *Bhagavad Gita* and other religious texts picked up from the bookstore—all that I started reading, mixed with the images my family had prevailed on me as a child. And Shakuntala, Hanuman, other deities including favourites such as Rama and Sita, and what else stemming from the triumvirate of Brahma, Vishnu, and Shiva. Vishnu holiness entered me, yet elusive or evanescent. Next an image of rebirth and reincarnation. Oddly, in Canada I started to feel I was an exile.

I also read what famed writers, mostly English, said about India. TV images of India and Asia also came back to me, the Third World as a whole with its poverty, so haunting. And V S Naipaul, someone of my background . . . I contemplated his "area of darkness." But India's green revolution and industrialization were taking place. Yet would there be a culture shock for me in my going to India?

Fulfilment was what I sought, all in wanting to come to grips with my anxieties about place and destiny. And where was home? . . . For weeks prior to leaving for the Subcontinent, I'd wake up in the middle of the night in a cold sweat and shudder. The plane ticket in hand, which I looked at while counting the days, and strangely it was as if I didn't want that time to come. One dream or nightmare reappearing:

upon arriving in India, my luggage was quickly lost . . . a cab driver kept running away with it despite my frantic efforts to hold on to what was mine.

I'd wake up wondering about this for hours, so vivid were the images. Haunting!

In Bramalea, near the Toronto Pearson International airport, my brothers and other members of my extended family came to "see me off."

"What are you going to India for?" one asked, noting my anxiety.

"To find out."

"Find out what?"

The passion and allure of India, all that sometimes gripped my imagination. Didn't they understand?

"You will die there," one scolded, sounding macabre.

"I will not."

"Haven't you seen the poverty?"

"On TV, you mean?" The tentative drawing out, an unexpected ritual.

Planes droning overhead over Pearson—all coming or going, to and from all parts of the world, Europe and America, mainly.

"You better be careful," came the terse warning—they were now all immigrants in Canada, mixing easily with the Canadian-born. And Canada had assimilated them, they were thoroughly acculturated. My own Canadianness I reflected on from time to time; and I said I had taken the necessary shots to ward off malaria, Hepatitis B, and whatever else.

They kept looking at me, my suitcase close by.

Immediately I felt the urge to tell them about Gandhi's autobiography: had they not read it? Now I would visit India, to find out all there was to know.

They looked at me warily, then maybe indulged me.

One smiled and said he was indeed pleased that a member of the family was going to the land of our ancestors. Did I detect a smirk?

My mother, dour, appeared intrigued. A diehard Hindu, she regularly did her pujas in Bramalea—the town near the airport—with friends, neighbours, attending. I recalled my fears about her coming to live in Canada and coping with "western" ways. But she'd adapted well, becoming adept with the microwave oven and other gadgets around the house. Now I, her eldest, was going to India; and in her unlettered fashion I'd watched her studying a map, feigning interest in places such as Madras (now Chennai), Delhi, Agra (where the Taj Mahal was located), and elsewhere.

Immediately I wanted to remind them about the Indians back in the Caribbean: in Guyana and Trinidad mainly, our ancestors who had been brought to the region as indentured labourers over a century ago; that history with its *kala pani* (dark water), crossed on ships that resembled slave-holding caravels. Indians from the Gangetic Plain had been tricked into coming to work in the sugar plantations in South America and the Caribbean . . . a far land, I wanted to emphasize. The spirit of *jahaji bhai* (ship brothers) had been formed, as a kind of kinship, a way of surviving.

My brothers kept looking at me. And India no longer seemed exotic, as I braced myself for more of their taunts. And strange new sensibilities, erasing the old in Canada, mixed with weather: the winter and cold temperature emphasizing difference.

Together we ate the curried goat, with large helpings of basmati rice, which my mother had cooked—like our last meal. And maybe at the back of my mind was the thought that in India I would be eating vegetarian food only.

My mother looked at me askance, in her mute fashion. And to my brothers, I kept muttering about India's recent development. Didn't they meet other Indians in Toronto? Ah, from time to time they listened to popular Indian songs performed in Bollywood-made movies; and then the classical singers like Lata Mangeshkar, whom they might have watched with intrigue on TV shows.

I tried to conjure up more Indian movie scenes: the extravagant musicians and dancers; then the melodrama, dark, brooding, even Gothic, always eliciting abundant tears. And in Guyana I'd thought we were gradually becoming a creole people. We were West Indians.

Then Canada, also far away, sounded like Xanadu. All shifting grounds, I considered; and maybe I was different from everyone.

I was flying Lufthansa (Air Canada didn't go to Bombay, and I didn't want to take a chance with Air India because of fears of sabotage). My frenzied thinking: it'd be the farthest I would travel.

That dream or nightmare of losing my luggage again, akin to being stranded in no-man's land.

Muted farewells expressed. A tear falling down my mother's cheek, as we shook hands, embraced.

I began coughing. They too coughed. My brothers avoided looking at me in the eyes.

I tried to put on a bold face; I was going to meet family members from way back, despite a sketchy genealogy at best. Yes, names had been changed, the entire family's history erased because the British—the colonial power—had never kept proper records: they had no patience with the Indian names. The "indentured servants," as my forebears were called, were meant to simply replace the African slaves who had gained their freedom in the sugar plantations (many to become "bush negroes"). This was all the history.

"Goodbye," they muttered.

"Goodbye," I replied.

My mother's ashen face, and she intuitively knew more: that it was good I was going to India. My father who wasn't around; did he know I would be travelling to India one day?

*

New emotions akin to independence: my being away from the family. Strangely the weight of Canada seemed to close in on me the farther away I imagined going.

And indeed, I summoned the confidence of the Canadian going to the Third World, like a defence mechanism. I watched the other passengers of various backgrounds, many Indians among them. Maybe they were all going to India? Many to visit family and friends; and it was Diwali, the season of lights, and Sarswattie the goddess of light was also the goddess of learning. I didn't feel

77

moved; I wasn't that religious.

The Indian passengers, with their boisterous children, laughed loudly as we boarded the plane. Then the passengers became reserved, the children putting on their best behaviour. And some passengers were aid workers going to the Third World, I knew; others, academics, with detached expressions, only bent on research. I discreetly took in people's dresses, habits; and why was I really going to India? All indeed a long journey.

I fidgeted in my seat. Then I tried sleeping, with destiny seeming to be all, and again glanced across the aisle at the handsome Indian woman with lipsticked mouth, her round child next to her fretting and fussing with endless energy.

The Lufthansa flight stopover in Frankfurt was approaching: this was one of the best European airports, truly international. Now many of the passengers would depart in Germany, and new ones would join us. I gripped my carry-on bag, my Canadian impersonality, as it seemed, sustained. And vaguely as I watched the new passengers, many Indians, I thought of what I'd heard: that Indians took a part of India with them wherever they went, such being the Subcontinent's grip on their psyches; some even kept parcels of Indian soil in their homes in Canada, America, or Europe.

My mother would be more intrigued.

I focussed on an Indian family, the wife pregnant; dark eyed and beautiful. Next I made eye-contact with a portly middle-aged man, a seasoned traveller by the looks of it. He asking me what city I was going to on my return to India!

I told him it was my first trip there.

He quickly became impersonal; and his sari-clad wife looked at me doubtfully. Their two children, a boy and girl, smiled, then ran away to play in the sprawling Frankfurt airport waiting area.

Strangely I began to think I'd left Canada for good, that I'd become a foreigner . . . among all nine hundred million people there, without status or country; India seemed no longer the land of my ancestors.

European passengers among others boarding. More Indian passengers too, and children with doting mothers, fathers, scolding. "I told you not to run there!"

The pregnant dark-eyed, beautiful woman, with a tikka, the red dot on her forehead, cast a sideways glance at me. The other passengers in transit: the aid workers from Germany, Scandinavia, and Americans—all participating in the silent drama of etiquette.

My day-dreaming self: Canada, the Great White North, as I imperceptibly forced myself to consider a new identity. Was I still a Canadian? I might have fallen asleep, thinking I hadn't left Canada at all.

Was going to India just a long nightmare?

I quickly opened my eyes. The plane moving in space, and I conjured up the Indian Ocean and the Arabian Sea, all unknown worlds, a far galaxy.

The seat next to mine was empty, and after a while I lay down sideways and tried closing my eyes after becoming tired of reading. The movie didn't interest me; the music was monotonous. The food and coffee, drinks, all beginning to be punishing.

I forced myself not to imagine anything at all.

Was this possible? Yet an airport crowd in Bombay, all my lost relatives from generations ago, waiting to welcome me. Could this be possible?

The fellow in the aisle seat not far from mine, which was next to the window stirred; he'd embarked on the plane in Frankfurt, and he'd switched seats, to come closer to me. Sameer, about twenty, handsome, plump body, with a gold bangle on his left wrist; his clothes were stylish, in a young-people sort of way. He smiled. The pretty flight attendant held his attention, and he was asking her if she was Indian. "Are you?"

Dark she was, working for Lufthansa: an anomaly.

Sameer fiddled with his Indian passport on the small, pull-out table before him. She politely told him to pull up the table: the plane was experiencing turbulence. "Wait a while," he said, with a rolling shake of his head, looking rather benign.

She walked away, then deliberately returned. Yes, she must wait until he was finished contemplating his passport before he pulled up the table.

We made eye contact; and Sameer, well, he seemed bashful, or was just unmindful of me. I introduced myself.

He told me he'd been to London on a short holiday. He had friends there. Soft-spoken, his expression continually mild, endearing even. He attended a commercial college in Bombay. Then he looked at me appraisingly for the first time. Again he fiddled with his passport. I imagined him as a young Bollywood movie-star type; the few Indian movies I'd watched came back to me in a flash. And the plane would soon land in India, I thought. Would I see the Ganges River if I looked down, looked hard enough?

Sameer's amiability grew, as I kept imagining the subcontinent as once a huge island, but which had drifted into the mass of Asia. How real?

Sameer became solicitous, vaguely enquiring about my background; but not about Canada. The flight attendant again walked by, the same swarthy-complexioned, petite one. Sameer figured she was Indian, nothing less. Then, in answer to my questions, he told me his father was a millionaire. He said this blithely. He'd go into business after he graduated, he smiled again.

We ate our European vegetarian food: distinct from Indian vegetarian. Sameer was glad to return home, he said, during Diwali, though it'd be firecrackers everywhere. He laughed. Yes, he liked Bombay: he could live nowhere else; he'd never emigrate. He had many friends in London, too; but he partied a lot at home: he and his friends going to clubs, discos, both sexes in Bombay (he called it Mumbai). He liked things Western; and things Indian as well. We talked about cricket, the most popular game in India. Yes, he admired the Indian player Sachin Tendulkar, who was from Bombay. Pride lit up his eyes.

I also smiled. Our camaraderie, or what seemed like it, growing.

India's mystique or exoticism was disappearing. Tell my brothers this. I laughed. Sameer grinned.

Why I also wanted him to show interest in Canada, I didn't know; I wanted him to ask about snow, and about my living in the Great White North, and the adjustments I'd made over the years. Maybe to even ask if I was indeed born in South America. Possible?

Instead, he looked around uncomfortably. He was again looking for the flight attendant.

I told him I expected to be greeted at the airport in Mumbai: my host would send her driver, at two in the morning; the driver would have a placard with my name on it; large, bold letters, I imagined.

Sameer sensed my anxiety. He said not to worry.

I showed him my host's address in , a suburb of Mumbai. I unfolded a small map of India. Mumbai suddenly seemed a conglomeration of districts, places: so confusing. Again Sameer said not to worry.

Then he began telling me of the Maharashtrians who lived in Bombay, about their spirit and determination over the years, centuries . . . Maharashtrians were a warrior sort, and vaguely he talked of a great warrior named Sivaji, who'd terrorized the Mogul invaders. I listened keenly. Next, he talked about the Portuguese, the British: all that past. Then about the many ethnic groups, languages in India's largest city; and should I tell him I knew a Parsi writer born in Mumbai now living in Canada?

Mumbai was cosmopolitan, Sameer emphasized, as I visualized nightclubs where he and his friends danced under strobe lights, disco-style. But Mumbai was also polluted and overpopulated, he hinted, though nonchalantly. It was no problem.

My Canadian concern over ecology . . . thirty million people back there, all residing on tundra, snow-laden ground, far unlike the blistering heat and humidity of Mumbai, and the inevitable monsoon floods, to come. Again I conjured up my brothers' faces, and my mother's, all perhaps wondering if I'd arrived safely. An unending ordeal they might seem to think it was. And my landing . . . .and what happened next? Did they think I would meet someone like Sameer?

The petite flight attendant again: more professional, her smile unvarying.

The plane started descending.

All the other passengers seemed to start readying themselves for India, including the beautiful dark-eyed woman and her children, and the aid workers.

I reminded myself that I was an experienced traveller: I had been from coast to coast across Canada, from Whitehorse and Yellow-knife, to St John's, Newfoundland. Icebergs in my imagination, the same that toppled the Titanic. Landscapes, all coalescing. A great huge sky disappearing. A welcoming, maybe, my auspicious meeting. Arrival.

"Don't worry," said Sameer. The plane was touching down. "I won't worry," I assured him, thinking of an astrologer, somewhere, mumbling over his time-worn chart with signs, and other impressions, all awaiting me . . . India with its legions of esoteric beliefs.

I right then bolstered the thought that I was a Canadian entering a foreign land. This was no mere defence mechanism. History dispensed with: indenture, kala pani, vanished. The flux of time and change, only. I was a Canadian.

Sameer laughed, as the petite flight attendant caught his attention again. Would he now ask her once more if she was Indian? But he only fiddled with his passport. I fiddled with mine too, my heart racing.

Landing in Mumbai, Sameer was calm, a seasoned traveller. Now he, the experienced one, though I vaguely thought I was the one who'd been across the United States, Cuba, the rest of the Caribbean, the United Kingdom, Europe.

On veritable Indian soil, I was, in the land of Mahatma Gandhi, Nehru, and Sivaji; and Bollywood movie stars, and the Taj Mahal, a timeless symbol of love created by Shah Jehan; and Kipling and the British East India Company. Here indeed, the "bright jewel in our crown of Empire"—Queen Victoria, remember? The viceroy and vicereine who'd settled in Shimla in the foothills of the Himalayas to escape the unbearably stifling heat of Delhi during the summer. Here, where my ancestors had come from, taken more than a century ago to work in the sugar plantations close to the Amazon and Orinoco.

With more than instinct I followed Sameer, keeping close to him as much as possible.

Deliberately, he kept looking back at me, in the line going out. Would he one day be a big tycoon and perhaps come to Canada to do a business deal?

The particular flight attendant seemed to have disappeared.

"Follow me," Sameer commanded.

The airport at two in the morning was hot, humid.

Crowds outside, and the air I breathed in, distinctly Indian, if somewhat oppressive. Outside, through the wide-open doors, I tried to see my name, on a placard, raised high somewhere.

Auto-rickshaws and taxis everywhere, cacophonous, the air sweeping across the Arabian Sea. More horns blaring. Where was Sameer? Passengers, with relatives all hailing in the medley of greetings. It was an auspicious time to fly, the astrologers were correct.

I started going through Immigration, Customs. Passport held firmly. And I was indeed a Canadian, in a vast new land. Something else I recalled: the time when I'd first arrived in Trudeau's Canada more than two decades ago. Sensations of heart and mind, at the Toronto International Airport. The two lines for incoming passengers: one for residents of Canada, and the other for foreigners. I was one of the latter, dutifully finding myself in the right line, and wondering if I'd be admitted into Canada!

Much later when I'd travelled abroad and returned to Canada, I'd felt this dread again: like a throwback in time. Now here in Mumbai, standing next to the other passengers, including foreigners, the aid workers, researchers . . . there was only one line. My jetlagged body, my feelings, and the heat stifling. I yet mustered my Canadian confidence.

An Indian policeman, khaki-clad with shorts, carrying a truncheon or club, stood alongside to guide the line along in an orderly fashion. He was a far cry from the burly Canadian type, being about my height. Where was Sameer?

I felt tall, taller than the mustached policeman. What line must I go to? And I was a foreigner, didn't he know? I approached him. My Canadian bravado now, remember? "Excuse me," I said, looking down the line.

He waited.

"Where do I go to?" I looked around. "I'm not, well . . . Indian." The sense of the Canadian, the Great White North fully in me; the cold and ice in my veins, in my living in Canada for over twenty years.

Oddly, it seemed too I was in no-man's-land. And my brothers', and my mother's warnings about India, encapsulated in this moment. And the nightmare of my luggage disappearing!

The policeman looked me up and down, slowly. Quizzically. My complexion, demeanour, seemed to fascinate him; and my words yet reinforcing my no-man's-land status, yet my being strangely Canadian.

Then with a shake of his head, in characteristic Indian fashion, the policeman smiled, and blurted: "Don't worry, we're all Indians here!"

Yes, I was in India: I had returned, remember?

I also smiled.

Sameer joined me, grinning because he thought he'd lost me. He began seeing me through Customs, like a long-lost brother, welcoming me anew. We're all Indians here!

The dark-complexioned flight attendant from afar also smiled. But Sameer seemed to ignore her. He was only concerned with me.

My father in faraway Guyana, I vaguely thought about. Now I didn't think of my brothers and mother in Toronto.

Sameer started looking for my name in the crowd outside with everyone seeming to be waving, placards, banners, lifted high; all with names written in mostly spidery Hindi script.

He pointed. My name, in small letters, on a tiny placard or billboard at the far back, written in crisp English. I was relieved. Sameer laughed.

We shook hands.

Horns blaring, everywhere, all across India at once. And I instinctively recreated my first time arriving in Canada and pretending to hear the Canadian security guard saying, "Don't worry, we're all . . ." The words I would write to my father now, then to my mother in Toronto.

The chauffeur of the car—my host's—hooted a thousand times. Firecrackers everywhere. Diwali celebrations, maybe. My luggage hadn't as yet disappeared. When I imagined seeing the petite flight attendant once more, I immediately thought of Sameer playing with his passport, and his longing to return to India. Nowhere else!

# Tḥe Macḥine

W iry, gnarled, and well over sixty Nanna was, but still going strong. He preoccupied me more than usual, as he fretted and fumed, and everyone else seemed puzzled by his mood. "He goin' crazy," one scoffed, machete rising against cane bark. Nanna yet whirring, as he would be again the next morning, walking along the winding road and then going with others on the truck to the cane field; and there was no point chaffing him now: the young school teacher that I'd become.

Nanna's muscles tensed as he raised his machete in the air. Whack! He hit the cane bark hard. Then he started muttering that people didn't have to do this work. Why not a machine? I imagined his lips throbbing, as the others laughed; and maybe they knew something I didn't.

"Such a machine impossible, ol' man," cried one, grinning.

Nanna pulled another bundle of cane across his narrow shoulder and sucked in the dry air. With a grunt he threw the bundle into the large iron punt, with a heavy clang. And he continued thinking of that machine, metal grooves on his forehead. And I imagined leaving here for England or America, where I'd make a name for myself; I'd never remain here to cut cane like Nanna, or the rest of them.

Whack! I heard again.

Nanna and Grandma (his sister) hardly saying much to each other, a weird fate or destiny keeping them apart: the same that brought their parents to these shores a long time ago. I'd watch Nanna sometimes read the holy book, the Ramayana: the battered-looking copy of the Indian epic in the family: the pages frayed, yet it was special here in this far place, Guyana. Grandma also looking at him, dwelling on ancestry. Cymbals crashing, tabla drums in the celebration of holi. Phagwah.

Nanna's face narrow, eyes yet gleaming.

Grandma, somewhere else, resplendent in a sari, looking beautiful. These thoughts humming in my mind.

Nanna started making his way home after the day's work was done. Looking at him from the window of our house built on stilts—with Grandma next to me—I wondered about the machine he'd kept talking about; he wanted to find out more about it: such possibilities maybe. Old as he was, he seemed preoccupied more and more each day.

"It's something else on his mind," Grandma muttered.

"Something else?" I looked at her doubtfully.

Grandma, fidgety, wagged a finger at me as I braced myself for her scepticism.

Nanna coming closer, his hands throbbing.

"Why he not give up cutting cane?" Grandma said. "Maybe he will work until he drop dead." Nanna, coming closer, soot scarring the corners of his nose, mouth. Immediately I waved to him.

Slowly he waved back.

"How was it today?" I asked when he was within earshot.

Grandma watching discreetly from a chink in the window.

"Still thinking about that machine?" I asked, doubt in my mind.

Sometimes he humoured me, his aquiline nose twitching as he shrugged, the yak bag slung across his shoulder: the same carrying the aluminum saucepan often containing his regular fare of rice and vegetables fried with masala. A cutlass (machete) was slung across his left shoulder. His eyes held me to his. "So you hear?" he asked.

"Yes." I moved down the balcony to be close to him. "I've been making enquiries, looking in magazines, books," I added.

"Books?" He didn't believe in books, those intimidating words in English like hieroglyphics.

His eyes shifted to the window. Maybe Nanna felt he was betraying the legacy of hard work: a pact his forebears had made with the plantation owners. Was a machine really an easy way out? Ah, Grandma watching him, their silent communication, mixed with rage. He rubbed the back of his neck where the skin itched. Blood oozed.

Before long he would reach his small house half a mile down the brick road where he'd go to the standpipe and wash away the soot from the burnt cane from the pores on his skin. A smile would creep across his mouth. The next day it would be the same again, the others in the cane field still watching him with doubt, I figured.

"I hear in Cuba they got such a machine," I said.

"Cuba?" He raised his head at an angle. "Where is Cuba?" He was ashamed of his ignorance.

Our politicians sometimes talked about Cuba, though Nanna hardly ever listened to them. Once he'd said, "What's the use?" Now I wanted to tell him about Cuba, other places, or history: about invasion and conquest. As a young school teacher I was supposed to know everything; and about sugar cane being harvested in other places, in the Caribbean, Africa, the Far East. Nothing seemed real anymore.

Nanna started walking away, a gust of wind now carrying him along. He wouldn't go to the standpipe to wash now, but simply fall into his hammock and mutter phrases from the Ramayana: all perhaps stored up in him from a long time ago. And did he again think about India where his father and mother had come from? Eyes closed, he'd also mull over what I said: about other places, origins. And about that machine to cut the cane: his obsession.

Then he'd fall into a deep sleep, still recalling images of a past when he and Nanni (Grandma), and other sisters and brothers lived with their parents in this "far land."

Grandma and Nanna, as children, skirting the coastland bushes close to the village. Heavy brush, trees, not far from the large acres of sugar cane: in the wayward plantation. Grandma and Nanna's parents, newcomers to this forbidding land, set to clear the virgin brush from early morning to night. All the while they kept sustaining themselves, vying with other customs and traditions; the children frolicking . . . the parents now gone for most of the day.

The subcontinent's astrologers consulting fanciful charts, nattering away about the stars and a holy river named Ganges . . . while far away workers kept doing the daunting work in a land once called El Dorado. The children climbing up the guava tree, vicariously challenging the Bengal tiger that prowled, as the elders jabbered away in Hindi. African pidgin or patois in the air; and who or what were they becoming?

The surprising pounce of the beast, with a loud cry of fear coming from their lips in their new creole tongue. Let the plantation owners with their managers and overseers from England listen to them now!

Still mimicking their parents' worshipful chants, the children stood before many-armed, many-legged gods and goddesses: Arjuna, Krishna, Ganesha, the elephant-headed one. Incense burning. Cymbals crashed in a strange voodoo-and-calypso-crazed world, all still celebrating the abolition of slavery. A tabla punctuated a voodooienne's cry. Lotus drifting down a monsoon-driven river, really far away.

The machine was making solid grooves on the squelchy ground, and why did I have to tell Nanna that in Cuba such a thing existed? Such a thing that could only be invented by someone who was a mechanical genius.

Chiaroscuro patterns on Grandma's face too, because of light darting across the wall in my room. She too couldn't sleep, she said, the wall lamp flickering, dappling her cheeks. A silent, mute communication between us; and the language of indenture, with her dead parents still somewhere around, I imagined. My thoughts drifting to my own mother and father, all in my new Elvis Presley and Patsy Kline interest, or my wanting to be a Harlem dude in zoot and yearning to be in America. Reggae rhythms with images of an elusive Babylon also coming closer.

Grandma quietly started leaving the room, the Ramayana's images in her mind in the night's long requiem.

And the next day, Nanna wouldn't go to work; I didn't see him pass by. The workers chopping the cane, in my daydreaming. "It's that machine he still thinkin' bout!" one hurled.

"Or he stayin' home to invent this machine," sniffed another.

The crash of a dozen cane stalks in the bright sun. Then swiftly tied into a haphazard bundle, an expert job done as sinewy arms folded the cane, the workers heaving, lifting the bundles and taking them to the cane punt.

"You mean he really stay home?" asked another, wiping a swathe of ash from his face.

"Maybe he sick."

Others picked up the refrain: "Yes, he sick?"

"Don't forget he old, he not young like we." Perspiration like resin stuck to their necks, hands.

"Not strong like we," emphasized another.

"But he gat India-coolie blood!" came a snappy retort.

The African workers conjuring up their own elusive ancestry with a sense of Yoruba pride, here faraway from the so-called dark continent. Another said, "What if the old man not wake up again? What if he's . . . well . . . dead?"

"That man too strong. He go live up to a hundred," came a sustained hiss. "He's still thinking about that machine."

"How can a machine without hands put cane together, and to tie cane bundle?" argued another, a strange mood overtaking them.

"And be able to put bundle neat-neat in the punt like we do?"

Another rasped that in a movie he'd seen such a machine.
"Impossible."

A new challenge as they huddled together: "Is only white people
can invent such a machine, na?" The name "Australia" was mentioned, a place close to India: which started another round of argument. "Black an' brown people never can invent such a thing."

Tremor in my veins the more I imagined, as a further challenge
hung in the air.

Whatever the machine was, man had to assist it, they rallied. And
no machine worked alone, not by itself. "Will they bring it from England then?" asked Ragbir.

Maybe Nanna knew the answer, another offered, with a mystery
still growing about the old man; and one or two looked at me with
suspicion later that day as they recreated the discussion. I told them
"Old people like that sometimes know things."

"They do?"

"But where is he?"

Aside, Grandma said, "You mustn't talk much wid them." She
wanted me to be different. The cane-cutting "boys" now idled at our
cakeshop when the harvesting season was over.

"Why not?" I retorted.

Grandma's refrain: "Rememba, you're differen'."

"I'm not different," I said.

"You are. Now you mus' listen to me!"

"I am a teacher," I hurled. "It's hard work to make children learn."

"It's not like cutting cane, eh?" she laughed.

"Teaching's working with your brains. I write things on the black-
board; I make the children learn," the words rushed out.

Grandma seemed pleased I said that, though she added, "So they
could leave here one day?" Was she somehow thinking of Nanna
again?

I had to see Nanna again, though I imagined him laughing, saying,
Well, what does it matter? A strong wind was blowing all across the

*91*

narrow coastland, though I also imagined an awfully cold breeze in a far-off place; then a machine ploughing through fields, slashing through the cane and threshing it with knives that were like monstrous teeth. The machine next nudging the punts along the network of canals to the factory.

Ah, where was Nanna? There was no sign of him coming along the main road. "See, I too could travel; it's not only you wid your education," I imagined him saying, dressed in jacket and tie, dignified-looking, the same Nanna who never went beyond the district, tied as he was to the plantation ground in a pact made since the time of indenture.

I continued thinking of that special machine, then about the workers enjoying a holiday since the target set for harvesting the cane would soon be met. Nanna indeed among those going to far-off places, wouldn't he?

I saw Nanna coming down the main road, face not blotched with soot, or tired-looking as before. I hurried down the stairs to meet him, the entire balcony coming down with me. "I hear you've been sick," I let out. He shook his head; he hadn't been sick. "You're not working anymore?"

He was taking a long time to answer. "I'm an old man," he frowned. I waited to hear more, breathless. "Cutting sugar cane is for young people; not for me, son." A smile wreathed his mouth, and he seemed ready to move on. Yet he waited.

"Is that why you've stayed away these last few days?"

He mumbled something, amused by my questioning. Then it dawned on me: Nanna had actually gone to see the managers; to tell them about this special machine. Tell them too about the hardship since indenture, and he'd had enough of it; and about his mother and father who'd come from a far place, India. Now a machine must cut the cane. Human beings couldn't keep doing this work forever.

Maybe he'd referred to me, saying I—the young schoolteacher—knew of such a machine. It existed in Cuba. The foreign managers laughing their heads off as he gesticulated. Oh, how they laughed.

Looking at Nanna, I waited to hear more.

Others coming around to hear him talk, incredible as it was that he'd indeed confronted the managers: he who could hardly read or write, though he was far from illiterate. He read the Ramayana, didn't he? And Grandma was also looking from the window, I figured. Now was the time for reconciliation between them, because of the Ramayana they shared: the one copy, like a relic, often kept in a bottom drawer for safety.

Nanna wagged a finger at me, as if now reneging on the past. Grandma still at the window, and maybe she knew where he'd been as she kept remembering vivid details of the past. Details of a ship in a wild ocean, the waves rising a thousand feet high! Nanna started walking away, quickly.

Grandma's face with shadows dappling it because of the sun. And faster Nanna walked. The boys, in predictable fashion, calling out: "Old man, where are you going now?" Then, "Tell us where he's been, Teach!" they said, looking at me.

I shook my head, I couldn't tell.

"Tell us!"

I stammered, incoherent.

They insisted, "Tell us, see."

I answered vaguely, and they instinctively mocked, saying I was the teacher who was supposed to know everything and didn't!

Others chorussed, "The overseers from England, they will bring this machine that could grunt an' talk like us, no? That could swear like us too, ha!

"They go bring it right into the field, this machine that will feel a burning pain on its skin. One that could sweat too, and its skin go stink wid all de soot and mud! Yes, a machine that would lift a whole bundle of cane close to its breast, and heave it onto its shoulder. Such a machine . . . that only foreign people could invent!" It was as if Nanna was doing all the talking now.

"It'll make noises in the field too, an' laugh and really get belly-ache an' stomach-ache. Maybe they go feed it dhal an' rice, and plantain like African people does eat. Heh-heh-heh!"

I looked at their faces, their strangely bewildered expressions. "Yes, a machine we will keep looking out for," said Govind, the most talkative among them. "It will wave to us from a distance, giving us ease from this hard work. We'll start taking holidays too, like foreign people an' travel everywhere." Their voices rose.

"And when we come home we will be talkin' 'bout the places we've been to; and the machine will laugh. Really laugh!"

I started running down the street to where Nanna lived, the voices pushing me along. Grandmother coming behind me.

Suddenly I felt Nanna was no longer around. A tremor took hold of me when I reached his house. I knocked on the door.

No answer, or sound.

Grandma close by, the two of us alone; her face florid because she'd been trying to keep up with me. Fear also entered her eyes.

I slowly pushed the door open . . . and I knew at once.

Grandma lowered her head; in silence, she hissed, "He . . . dead!"

A machine's mute whir, somewhere, a sound I kept hearing, and seeing. Nanna's ashen face: like the old man he was. Or wasn't. Sounds accompanying my laboured breathing.

Grandma breathed hard also, as I watched her picking up the battered-looking Ramayana on the table and lipping words from it.

Waves beating in an ocean; the new currents in a far time or consciousness; and everything locked in memory was now being slowly released, unravelling too as we travelled (I imagined) more and more.

# Who Is Lee Harvey Oswald?

They are drinking beer at the corner of Burnside Avenue not far from Grand Concourse in the heart of the Bronx, the Budweiser bottles concealed in brown paper bags with their heads sticking out like nipples. "Hey, Manlall, what's the matter?" a voice calls.

Manlall's lips stretch like rubber, as he grunts a reply. He sucks at his beer next, shifting his gaze down the street and thinking of when he first came to America almost thirty years ago: on the very day President John F Kennedy was shot. The plane flying overhead, and Lee Harvey Oswald was aiming a rifle at JFK, come to think of it. Bone-thin Manlall was then, and a clarion voice in his head: Come all you weak, famished, downtrodden from everywhere, including Central and South America, Eastern Europe, Russia, Mexico, the Caribbean. Come to Ellis Island. Now genuflect before the Statue of Liberty as you shed your rags and dream of getting rich one day in America!

Manlall guzzles his beer, wondering why he'd left the South American coastland where he was born, where he used to spray poison in the cane fields to eradicate pests: mainly rats damaging the crops, while the foreign overseers drank scotch and concocted schemes of improving the sugarcane yield and how best to run black people's lives.

"Manlall, drink up," another shouts. "You think you're more American than the rest o' us?" Voices in apartment buildings in the Bronx, Queens, Brooklyn, all amidst further images of rats with beady eyes running helter-skelter.

"It's here where we're now, Manlall," shrieks another.

Sucking at his Budweiser, Manlall—short-bodied, with a slight paunch—the beer going down his throat in gulps, starts coughing. "Don't kill you'self, man," he hears, laughter following.

"Eh?" Manlall jerks his head back, at an angle with the paper bag. Eyes focussing on three tawny-looking teenage girls in red, yellow, and pink on the opposite side of the street littered with empty Export 'A' and Players cigarette packets, and discarded tabloid newspapers proclaiming New York City the murder capital of the world. Well, no more!

Manlall's mind is working at top speed: the subways are now safe, but a man can't easily walk around, unlike the forested place he came from more than two decades ago. The Guyana Airways jet overhead—that day he first arrived—and the shocked scene at the airport because of the assassination of the President. "Drink up—you're in America," another fella shouts mindlessly.

The girls turn, smiling, teeth glistening in the sun, as Manlall looks at them with unaccustomed concentration.

"So, what's on your mind?" rasps another in their ongoing palaver.

Olive skins and browns blend in the heat across the street. Gloria—he has seen her before—coquettishly throwing her head back as she looks at him. A scurrying pace in his mind amidst Latino-tropical rhythms, the summer heat biting into his neck. Again he puts the bottle to his mouth, savouring the taste. Stop it, fellas. Stop it, for God's sake!

"We're with you, man," another hurls. "We don't carry guns cause we're now law-abiding immigrants in America!"

The brown bag crisp against his lips, Manlall looks at Gloria, at her largish eyes, and he feels he knows her: has seen her around. Yeah, leave the Bronx to us. Leave it only to Americans. Voices he keeps hearing.

Manlall's mouth twitches, more beer going down his throat like bitter gall, the Budweiser bottle held firmly in his hand. A frenzy in his spirit, too, and he's not sure any longer why he's in America; not sure why he's in the Bronx, when he could have been somewhere else, maybe in Louisiana or Miami. Or Toronto. All dreams he once had; and the image of flying into America when the announcement was made in the plane by the captain in the cockpit: "I have some terrible news to report . . . " Is the plane going to crash? "President John F Kennedy was shot in Dallas, Texas, a few minutes ago." It can't be true. Christ, I am flying into America!

—You's all alien, ya know—he hears, the Budweiser still in his hand.

—Gloria, shut the fuck up!

Manlall walks up and down the block close to Ryer Avenue, studying the grey apartment building before him like a huge box; here where they nicknamed him "The Mayor." Unflinching he is, yet thinking hard. All about the pandemonium in America on that day Kennedy was shot.

"See, one day you will replace Mayor Giuliani himself, won't you?"

Will I?

The familiar old woman with distinctly tar-black lips protruding, sitting on the front porch of the Ryer Ave apartment building called "The Rock": she's keeping watch on everyone going by, having done this for a decade or more. She croaks to herself: "Mayor, Mayor . . ." sounding like "Mirror, mirror."

Squinting in the sun, Manlall takes it all in, including Gloria flaunting herself, shapely behind and all. More echoes in his mind, with the heat now an overpowering sensation.

"We've made it big here. We have all the social life we want," hoots another.

"They're all ethnics," murmurs the old woman sombrely.

Manlall believes it's now the hottest time of the year in the Big Apple. "Say, is it true President Kennedy was shot the day you came to America?" the old woman—a genuine American as she is—asks.

"You helped us get our green cards, man. Now West Indians are everywhere, becoming true citizens of America. We're not just crack-and-cocaine users, yeah," cries another, like madness taking over.

Manlall again looks across the street, focussing on Gloria as she moves with a cantering stride, her hips rising. He notices the others start closing in on her. "Is she the Marilyn Monroe of your dreams?" Oooh!

Is Gloria thinking of the boyfriend she's left behind in San Juan? The day she's planning to wear white and be the nuptial queen of all she surveys, confetti scattering in the air as she holds on tightly to her handsome, mustachioed beau. The image keeps growing in Manlall's mind. Next he imagines being the groom himself, escorting her and lifting her across the threshold to his door. Rats scurrying, tropical cane fields burning.

"She only keeps pretending to belong here in New York," hisses the old woman.

Does she?

"Who's really an American anyhow?" she scoffs cynically, looking around.

Manlall takes in the old woman's incessant lamentation: her almost time-worn ABC voice coming again at him. "Hey, Mr Mayor, go out and have fun. It's always the way of you immigrants!" Is she indeed a former ABC anchorwoman?

"Americans are elusive, as much as our destiny is," he hears next. "I've lived long enough to know what I'm talking about." She keeps muttering mindlessly.

*

A police car is moving along, easing in. The blonde woman at the wheel frowns, as the fellas quickly start concealing beer bottles in

wide coat pockets. The cop-woman's hard expression, uncompromising glare. Black, brown, and yellow faces grimacing, even while
some are playing cards and clapping dominoes close by. Rhapsodic
laughter follows. Hands chop the sultry air in the heat. "You can't escape it, it's the American way," mutters the ABC voice. "The cops
know everything." A gap-toothed warning, her face gashing a smile.
"They have too much computer stuff in those cars nowadays. It's
what the modern age's all about."

Manlall notices Gloria's eyes following the car. Then she starts
running. For God's sake, don't! The police car accelerates, swerving
at an angle with a loud screech. Tires burning. Manlall's heart beats
faster.

The ABC's woman's voice: "Don't trust anyone. I've been in this
neighbourhood long enough to know."

"Gloria, stay put!" Manlall rasps.

A flutter of paperbags. Gloria, it's true: I came to America on the
day JFK was assassinated. A further screech, brakes. Then the cop
dashes out, racing after Gloria and grabbing her.

Gloria is now a tigress, fighting back. "Leave me fucking well
alone, you pig! I know my rights!"

The words echoing: Get your black ass in line; show respect for authority, for American power. I will put the cuffs on you so tight your
wrists will bleed, burn and ache. America must be protected from
scum like you!

Manlall waits for other voices to punctuate the air. But no other
sound comes now.

Nothing.

Then the ABC voice calls out again from the corner of Ryer and
Burnside avenues: that a young woman, a known dope addict, was ar-
rested at the scene of the crime.

Applause follows, like mimicry: "It's me you want. They don't call
me Mayor for nothing," he hears his own voice talking. His own con-
science, too, telling him who he is, why he is here.

"Your type's bringing America to ruin. You will destroy this neighbourhood," adds the cop. "Puerto Ricans, Jamaicans, and all those from Colombia, Honduras, Nicaragua, Grenada, Iran, Turkey." The cop's eyes are quartz, as she looks across the street at Manlall. The ABC voice drones on: "Drinking in a public place is against the law, don't they know? The cops are now in control in New York, you see."

"Stop harassing her," Manlall cries out to the cop.

"I'm simply doing my job."

"Like hell you are!"

"We must get rid of all the pimps, dope-pushers, crack and cocaine addicts from this neighbourhood." A finger pointing at Gloria. "All the carriers of AIDS, too! It's the Mayor's orders."

"What Mayor? Who's the real mayor around here? See, she has rights like everyone else."

"She's an alien."

"She was born in Puerto Rico."

"Not Panama or Colombia?"

"She needs help, a drug rehab clinic."

"Isn't she from El Salvador?"

"I won't help you convict her."

"I will put her in the slammer until she sobers up."

"Just like that?" Manlall snaps his fingers.

*

Fellas are still talking, asking: "They can't deny her her rights. She's no carrier of AIDS."

"Besides, she isn't carrying a sawed-off shot gun or grenade."

"Christ, no judge can haul her away from here just like that. It's America the free, dammit!"

"The issues are still about race and colour," Manlall sneers.

"We have a middle class to protect," says the ABC voice with a drone.

"Not a police or military class?"

Gloria's eyes move left and right, muscles tightening in her arms, thighs. Sisters, brothers, feminists, Democrats, Reverend Jessie Jackson . . . help me.

—Bitch, get the fucking cuffs off me!

—It's for your own good.

—I know what's good for me, cop!

—You must obey the law.

—Now I want to see my lawyer.

With Gloria in the back seat, the police car starts moving forward. The ABC voice is now like a familiar refrain: *"This afternoon an arrest was made at the corner of Burnside and Ryer Avenues. A young woman, a known dope addict . . . "*

—Man, you'd think we're in Central America with a police death squad just around the corner.

—This is the US of A.

Gloria is still protesting her innocence, screaming that she doesn't want to come face-to-face with another stern judge. She doesn't want to be put in a slammer here in the Bronx, or anywhere in America!

Reporters scribbling frenziedly, as if this is the last story they will ever write. All because of the public's need for high drama, don't you know?

—And form your own right-wing militia? So why not go to South Africa or Liberia to help eradicate crime?

(God, we're American citizens.)

Rats scurrying on soft ground after the tropical rain. Then the land seems to slowly rise. Leaves, foliage crackling, all that Manlall sees and hears. Burning the cane in the plantation is necessary before harvesting.

The police siren keeps sounding, with voices now raucous at every angle. The domino-playing and card-clapping crowd is everywhere, forming like a mob. Budweiser smells are still strong, despite the paper bags being crumpled.

—It's not like Canada, you see. Not like Toronto or Montreal—rasps another.

The fellas look at each other with bloodshot eyes. The ABC voice drones on again, though no one seems to be listening.

—What are you thinking, Mr Mayor? A penny for your thoughts.

Others now start walking to their cars parked in narrow spaces like peninsulas. Leeward and windward islands, too, with a hurricane wind not far off. And Manlall begins to feel he's in no-man's land now, yet imagines Gloria in a white bridal gown, and so lovely she looks. Everyone is now applauding.

The ABC voice again: *"A known dope addict will be getting married in New York City. The mayor will be walking with her along the aisle . . . "*

"When I was working for ABC in the olden days," the old woman continues, "I used to carry in-depth stories. Not like now with only the sound bytes that you hear. I used to research a story really well.

"Now everything's happening so fast. No one has the time to reflect on the meaning of why things happen, why events really occur. See, here there's no real neighbourhood anymore. Sometimes I feel I don't exist also."

Manlall feels a rope burning against his skin. The old woman's grandson is playing on a slope, skipping against a dull red wheelbarrow: which starts rolling sideways. Cars whiz past down Ryer Avenue, and Manlall's heart beats faster.

The old woman watches with half-blind eyes, adding, "I know what you're thinking, I can tell by your expression. The violence here is getting to you." She turns, observing her grandson inexorably moving towards the street on the wheelbarrow.

The boy's shout is a whelp of excitement. Instinctively the old woman waves at him. Manlall moves forward and tries pulling the wheelbarrow back to the lawn. But the kid scorns his attempt, laughing.

"Who's she really anyway?" the old woman asks with a nervous jerk of her head. Then she smiles and adds, "I'm getting on, maybe too old to see things clearly anymore. But ABC can still carry an in-depth story, you hear. Yes, Gloria, that's her name."

"Maybe Gloria's not her real name. Does she have a scar?"

"A scar?"

"You know her, right? Tell me, Mr Mayor, you do? Maybe you're looking for something all these years in America. It's why you came here, not just to have your dreams fulfilled, isn't it?"

"Dreams?" he shrugs.

The wheelbarrow is on the edge of the pavement, moving close to the oncoming traffic. "The judge will let her go, mark my words. They never keep them longer than a week." The wheelbarrow accelerates, and Manlall is about to reach out to it. The boy grins, as he is about to careen into the traffic.

"How times have changed," laments the old woman. "Ah, but nothing really changes, except people. We're talking about the death of a whole country, not just this neighbourhood." She wags her head, then looks at her grandson, as if transfixed.

When the boy tumbles, the entire building lurches forward into the street with him. The old woman impulsively lifts the tentacle of a hand, ambling forward. But Manlall is already wiping away spattered blood, touching the bruise on the child's left knee.

"This Gloria, you see, she used to live in this building. I used to see her all the time," adds the old woman, as the boy starts crying, mouth twisted. Manlall merely studies a small hill across a forked end where other streets converge. The kid makes as if to go to the wheelbarrow again. But the old woman quickly reaches out and pulls him back. "She doesn't come from here, though," she adds. "Maybe she's from your part of the world."

Manlall starts walking up the stairs of the apartment building, the Budweiser taste still in his mouth. He's thinking again of the day Kennedy was shot. His eyes straight ahead of the canting stairs. His boots easily graze against the steps. All other sounds, distances: he imagines. The plane coming down, about to land in America: and he's here for the first time. The cockpit voice again in his ears, all about President John F Kennedy being shot. No, it can't be true!

The police car comes forward; a siren wailing. Manlall feels the rage going through him, something really uncontrollable. The apartment door closes behind him. A loud bang follows.

The old woman twitches, grimaces. "Just like him to end it." She now stares at her grandson gripping the wheelbarrow again. She only breathes hard, listening for other sounds perhaps: another disaster about to occur, one that will truly break her heart.

# Marrying an American

On the phone she apologized—she said—for marrying an American. Her voice soft, controlled. "I had to." Then, "I'm sorry."
Reticence, the laconic quality in her voice. Now, after eight years, we
were talking again, amidst indifference stemming from distance because of our immigrating to other lands: she, to America; I, to Canada. Now it was like vestiges of time, refurbished. "No need to
apologize," I said.

Memory-words: as Sandi began recalling details of her family,
each member, all in her mind's eye. The turmoil of a familiar place;
and more people were leaving, didn't I know? I had taken out Canadian citizenship; I had no intention of returning there, I said. She
laughed, then reverted to a mutter, phrase: Ah, she was an American
now. The past unchanging. And slices of the village with place names
stemming from the English, French, Dutch. More memories altogether, like remnants, our village life: Adelphi, Reliance, Rose Hall . .
. the sugarcane plantation with molasses smells in the air, in the sun's
unrelenting heat. She was calling from Connecticut, didn't I know?

Oddly, we kept identifying ourselves to each other, like replaying
an old tape. She laughed again in an embarrassed way. "Are you sure

you remember me?" she asked. Maybe it was because our lives had become separate, distinct. I tried reconstructing the contours, then the fullness of her face, and it seemed time hadn't elapsed despite pot-sherd, grass, broken bottles, desiccated leaves: those details still vivid. Cowshit, sheep's, fowls' excrement. Then more voices in a sustained cacophony with a fully cadenced rhythm. Remembering also old forts, wharves, water lapping against greenheart in a coastland river. Then back to the present, like inevitably refurbished time again. "You see, I had to marry him," she added, her slow, half-hearted confession.

"I was all alone." Oh? "He's much older than me. He's Dutch, you see. But America's like that, with many races, people from all over the world . . . here." Why did she say that?

I heard noises coming from across the street. "We met in a piano bar," muttered Sandi. "He was by himself."

Her voice low, but steady. "I was shy, it was my first time there."

A click on the line, as if we were being recorded.

Yet I kept being intrigued.

"Then he smiled at me. Very friendly he was. He invited me over to join him for a drink. He needed company, he said. He too was shy." She stopped.

I urged her to continue on. She added: "He wanted to know where I came from. Hadn't heard about such a place, where I . . . we . . . came from." Pause. Then, "He knew I wasn't an American from the begin-ning." She giggled a little. "We promised to meet again," the words seeming rushed now. Then a laugh from deep down her throat came out. "He'd never been married before, he said."

It didn't matter now that she was chalking up an immense phone bill calling me long distance. Maybe Sandi's husband—this man— was wealthy. She lived comfortably. Ah, she simply wanted to talk now after all these years: the images floating up before us, all in her mind's eye; and mine as well: what we'd left behind and kept encoun-tering—always new beginnings. Now America was becoming mine. This man?

She wanted to know all that had happened to me over the years. "Please, you must tell me," she insisted. She grew tense. "I fell in love with Paul, though I was nervous, and afraid. What would people say . . . my family being what they are; and he being Dutch? Now I've started getting used to American life." She laughed nervously.

I remembered the boys in our village, in our growing up, all vying for her hand, their endless fantasies about her. She was attractive in a slim-waisted way; she used to walk twice a day to the village well, an aluminum pail balancing on her head, dark eyes flashing in the sun; sometimes she even looked stunning because of our tropics. And the boys chaffed each other about her. Who was really in love with her?

Who? One pointed to me.

They all did.

"Sandi, Sandi," they cheered and still pointed to me.

And she kept flaunting herself, with all her East Indian presence. Such breasts! And one called out loudly, "Prick-teaser!" Sandi said it was then that she started thinking about leaving.

The heavy pail on her head in a kind of balancing act, water dripping into her eyes. And America with huge highrises, skyscrapers, new and interesting people everywhere: she'd started thinking about. And the boys' insistent teasing: "When are you really leaving, Sandi? When?" Like mimicry, mixed with a strange pain and derision.

"Never?" She pouted, laughing at them also in the sun.

"You were born right here, and you'll marry one of us," another hurled, a lock of wavy hair sweeping across his forehead. Parody of all the village years rolled into one. A crotchety old woman, living down the street, who always whirled a coconut-branch broom with dust in the air, appeared in our line of vision. A vicarious hurricane coming also, as if the old woman willed, compelled it to happen after a long dry spell, we being so close to the equator. Trade winds combining with other coastal breezes, with the aromas of Bermuda grass, seashells, mullet, crab, mollusc. Then alluvium and topsoil, all solid imprints. Sandi's eyes lit up, her rebuke loud and long, "Leave me alone, all-you!"

"You will never go to America!" one of them replied, as if indignant. Was it I?

Yet another hurled, "Is a fat white American man you'll marry only! You will become his visa bride!"

"Or is it an American GI?" another heckled.

"None o' you!" she hurled back, distraught as she tossed a lock of hair away from her eyes, the pail still heavy on her head in her continuing balancing act. And how they longed to spend one night with her, fantasizing in unabashed glee.

And where was I?

What was I thinking?

The equator sun moving with a dreadful slowness, scorching, bright.

The telephone line crackled with static as Sandi slowly added, "I had to come to America, you see. What else could I do?"

I waited; and imagined something keeping us apart all these years.

Then: "Paul, he indeed said he loved me. He kept phoning every day." She talked on, desultorily, then finally said she'd fallen in love with him . . . all alone in America as she had been.

She emphasized, "I didn't want to return to the village. What for? To face them? " she scorned. "After four years, I became an American. Paul said America was now for us." I wanted to see her face, how much she had changed! I encouraged her to keep on talking.

She must.

I breathed in hard.

She did too.

This our meeting point, the telephone line crackling.

"Forgive me for going on like this," she said. "But we're happy together." She breathed in hard again. "You—I've been thinking about you too . . . you know." Voices in me, new impulses. It began to seem like more than five years since I'd left the South American coast, since I'd begun studying the ways of North Americans, especially Canadians. Life in the cities. Fast cars moving on strange highways, as I continually kept comparing here with there. And others kept coming to North America, not to England, leaving behind the bramble bush and black sage, to be here among the tundra, spruce, balsam, pine. Cold winds blustering across a large Ontario lake. The vantage point of high altitude, a plane moving among clouds in a dream world of temporary forgetfulness.

"Maybe you're the one I should've married," Sandi said next, surprising me. Maybe.

"So very sensitive you always were." She chuckled, as if embarrassed to say more. "It's true, I used to talk about you all the time. And Paul wanted to know who you were." She grinned, I imagined.

"I often imagine you in Canada living among Eskimos. It's true, no?" She again laughed, like a young schoolgirl. "I'm sorry to go on like this."

Now it was inevitable that I tell her more about myself. Was I happy? She sensed I wasn't.

Reluctantly I began talking about Deirdre. Who? Sandi's keen ear. Deirdre—a feminist—the woman I was now involved with; oddly, an American, Brooklyn-born; she often talked about her Jewish heritage, and about a grandmother who'd taken her skating in Madison Square Garden on Sunday mornings. I told Deirdre I dreamt of staring up at the Statue of Liberty: the entire dream was like that. She replied that all the world wanted to come to America! Canada—Deirdre added—was just a half-way point.

Such ease in Deirdre's words. She was attracted to me, she said, because of a restlessness in my spirit, similar to hers. She wanted me to speak to her in Spanish because I was a South American: I was exotic. I must continue to make her feel she was in some place else, not where it seemed like snow all year round. Yes, she longed to be Latin also. Deirdre and I would drive by the wealthy Rockcliffe Park area in Ottawa's east end, where the embassy crowd lived.

"No U-TURN," the large sign said. But Deirdre would swing her car around and cry out, "I've beaten the system!" Deirdre often talked about feminists such as Dorothy Dinnerstein, and about a minotaur mind-set. A strong lover in every white woman's life: like wish-fulfilment it seemed. Deirdre's sometimes Jungian preoccupations; and that year she'd spent in Zurich to plumb the fathomless depths of the unconscious. Psychoanalysis was all; and she'd become preoccupied with the daemon, and would one day write a novel about it. There were some things she wanted to work out of her system. Like death camps. Auschwitz. Tell Sandi more!

Deirdre said she'd easily overcome her fear of flying. Maybe she wanted men abundantly in her arms—even as she urged me to speak to her in Spanish.

I must! Not in English or French?

Would Sandi apologize again for marrying an American? Voices in the air, everywhere. Deirdre said she despised Canada because it didn't have a Bill of Rights with a First Amendment clause in it: one which she'd like to proclaim loudly in a Canadian courtroom. Just like the fascist bastard Oliver North did in Washington!

Deirdre had suggested that I move to San Franciso, I didn't belong in Ottawa. The city was too bureaucratic; and maybe too Wasp for me. I told her I wanted to live in the capital of the Great White North, to really experience it: and Ottawa was only two hours by car from an ethnic Montreal, and four and half from Toronto now with its own charged-up NBA team.

Deirdre simply laughed. Yes, nine hours from New York!

Fantasies ongoing. . .

"You will never marry her, I can tell," Sandi said next, with urgency and anxiety.

Deirdre had said she was starting to have multiple orgasms: and was it all she lived for? She'd accused me of being puritanical—a "Third World puritan." I needed to see a therapist, one who'd "tell you things about yourself, all that's repressed." Deirdre talked next about a Japanese lover she'd met in Europe, whose eyes were like quartz; he seemed imprinted on her mind.

"You were never the marrying kind," Sandi interrupted my thoughts. "Paul said he too was like that—he wanted to be single always. Until he met me, that is." She laughed harshly.

"Hartford, Connecticut, it's beautiful," she added, without waiting for an answer. "You must come and visit us. Maybe you don't travel to the US often. To New York maybe. But not to other places in America." She paused; she still wanted my approval in a way.

"This one you're in love with . . . ." she began, probing: as if she had all the time in the world. And Deirdre and I had come to the parting of the ways. Her academic interests were taking over, and she was anxious I didn't get "transferred onto her." When her Harvard friends came to visit, I became the outsider. She didn't want commitment; she was busy forming a Jungian Club in Ottawa with international connections. After our last date at the National Arts Centre to see opera, she charged that I'd stood her up. And that I was accusing her of wanting to castrate all men! "Nature abhors a vacuum," Deirdre cried to me.

Sandi said, "All the time I used to watch the girls here, the Americans. They go out with many guys: the ones I always see in the bars. Paul wasn't interested in them, only me. Because I was different, maybe old-fashioned." Again her laboured breathing.

Then with a soft shriek: "Did you see Mohan?" Yes, Mohan who'd taunted her loudest as she fetched the large pail of water in the village. "You remember him, don't you?" Mohan, often ribald; and she might have married him because she was starting to get "to that age": her parents now dictating an arranged marriage, weren't they?

"Mohan's still there; I keep hearing about him," Sandi added. Mohan, stubborn, never wanting to leave; never wanting to be called for the rest of his life a "new Canadian," an "ethnic" or an "alien." Married now, with four children.

I told Sandi all that I knew about him.

"It could've worked out between us," she said, nostalgic. Then, "But on a whim, I decided to leave for America." More laboured breathing. "Maybe one day Mohan will come here."

Canada? America?

Immigration laws, rules. Mohan once wanting to go to England (he'd also wanted to go to India): never to come to North America.

*111*

Obstinate, uncompromising Mohan once wrote to her, hinting that he was living in a large house with TV and video in every room; two cars: the same that America offered! Mohan, a village school teacher: his charges being children of poor sugar-estate workers, East Indians and Africans; and none was eager to learn in the sweltering heat, despite the parents wanting the best for them. Fifty kids in a classroom caterwauling, I imagined: Mohan shouting to them to behave. Yes, teach them by rote, arithmetic and spelling only. The sugarcane factory's incessant pound and grind in the harvesting season. Nerves raw, blood pounding.

Mohan laughing too, as he cried, "You must learn, arseholes!" Dialectal hiss. "What's the meaning of 'fasten'?" An African boy, in parody: "Like when two dogs fasten, sir!" That same afternoon, a parent crying out to Mohan: "When you too go leave, Teacher Mohan?" The jagged rhythm of cane stalks falling. Rice fields waterlogged. Men with machetes making wide sweeping arcs in the empty air. Mohan, spurning America, festering in his own hate. He'd become a Marxist overnight. Sandi, d'you hear?

Deirdre telling me it was good I was contemplating travelling in Europe: "In England, you'll see things differently." Adding that I'd be close to the vestiges of empire, Elizabethan and Victorian, and the Tower of London, images of Sir Walter Raleigh.

I imagined lying in a hammock under the house built on stilts in the tropics, wishing more of the trade winds to come and temper the heat. "Tell me, Kris, what you think about Europe when you return in a month's time." Deirdre urged, forcing an Ottawa Valley accent.

Sandi added that she was now encouraging her husband, the Dutch-born Paul, to take her to Europe too, to see the dykes, canals. Then she started talking about Canada again: Was it different from America? How was the crime rate? Drugs and senseless violence, and over two hundred and twenty thousand Americans carry guns in their homes, no? She let out a soft moan.

I told her Canada was a safe place. It was incredible, she exclaimed. I kept humouring her, as she wrested a promise out of me to call next. The tail end of our conversation: "I'm glad you approved," she finally said. Approved?

"I'm really happy to have called you. Once I got your number, I had to." Again her laboured breathing: "I hope you didn't mind. You'll really like him—Paul. You will, when you meet him!"

We kept on phoning each other, until that time when the calls no longer came. Then I figured I'd visit her one day in Connecticut: a surprise visit. But she said she and Paul would drive to Ottawa instead. He'd never been to Canada before: the Great White North. Perhaps she'd meet Deirdre too, she said. Ah, Deirdre and I were now simply two ships that had passed during the night. Sandi was uncomfortable with that image.

Now by coming to Canada she wanted me to see how "old" her husband was—and she laughed. Oddly, I imagined Paul to be really vigorous. And she seemed, strangely, small framed, birdlike. Was she the same one who'd balanced the heavy pail on her head in the village, when everyone had called out to her?

Deirdre smiling when I told her about Sandi not long after: saying it was good I was still in touch with "the tribe." And I would be sending her a postcard from the Tower of London, wouldn't I? Standing before Raleigh's chamber I would be contemplating the axe coming down on Ann Boleyn's slender neck.

Deirdre added, "You're resentful of me for breaking up the relationship. Men are always possessive."

"Are you still there?" asked Sandi at the other end, with the phone's static . . . in the air.

# Short-story Seminar

They are called Aravelli Hills, considered the world's oldest mountains, Professor Lall had said; and they are unlike the Himalayas, the world's youngest mountains. We kept going through the desert province of Rajasthan, heading for the pink city of Jaipur; and the bus had left New Delhi three hours ago, on a journey that never seemed to end. "I'm sorry to bring you to this," Professor Lall said, commiserating.

"Bring me to what?" I feigned not being fatigued, with a beating anxiety nevertheless. And maybe Professor Lall figured I'd be recording new sensations, experiences, all the while. Then the bus suddenly veered to the right, going off in the wrong direction, but no one seemed to mind because it would eventually find its way back to the main road: fate's compelling hand, nothing less, all bound to happen. A few passengers laughed, resigned to it all. I was also slowly becoming resigned to whatever occurred, yet with a lurking expectation, as Professor Lall somehow urged me to it.

Yawns everywhere, as if all of India was indeed yawning next to me. And among the passengers: scholars, writers and poets, a mixed assortment, all shaking their heads; and someone exclaimed next,

"Bhagwan!" God's name echoed, as if expecting the bus to capsize and go down a narrow bridge in gurgling waters below.

"I am sorry," again Lall muttered, and smiled.

I also smiled, and began thinking of myself no longer as the Canadian "guest": now feeling like one of the regular passengers heading for the "pink city"; and vaguely I wondered why Jaipur was called the "pink city," allowing my mind to come up with strange new images such as the colour of the earth itself being pink or red; and, more to the truth, the maharajahs having built stately pink edifices (palaces really) in a display of Indian opulence before the time of the Raj.

When the bus veered off again, I felt we were going everywhere across India all at once, despite a distinctive Rajput culture rising up around me. The gaudily decorated bus slowly turned round once more onto the main road, and some applauded. Sari-clad women passengers cheered, I watched, and a few of the men let out unexpected moans of happiness.

Large stretches of uninhabited land adjacent the main road I took in, interspersed with forest, as the bus went past, now in scarce light, as dusk slowly approached. Professor Lall, in jacket and tie next to me and looking like Dr Aziz in the movie *A Passage to India*, patted me on the shoulder. I concentrated on a small hut in the distance as I looked out from the window, and maybe desultorily conjured up Rudyard Kipling's Mowgli. And tigers in India also, the Bengal tiger no less; and what if one were to suddenly spring out from the forest floor and attack the person dwelling in his dim hut in the distance? Saffron light brightly shining, a glare of it. Maybe a sadhu lived in the hut, a fanatic bent on communing with his god, as the tiger kept stalking, coming close to his door! Would he imagine the beast to be an avatar of Vishnu, one of the gods, the spirit of holiness itself? "Think nothing of it," said Lall, smiling.

Oddly I complied, as the bus trundled on. The other passengers seeming more resigned, with the women hugging, embracing their nodding-off children. The men nattering, and maybe one or two might be imagining being the sadhu in the small hut we passed, even feeding the now benign tiger: indeed here where the most religious people on earth lived! And images of where my forebears came from; ah, but now I was living in Canada. "Think nothing of it," I thought I heard Lall say again, as if he once more guessed my thoughts.

The bus suddenly stopped with a jolt, something being amiss. One of the tires had gone flat, a back wheel no doubt twisted heavily against the constantly bumpy road. Indeed, already four hours had gone by since we'd left Delhi. Now the short skinny driver and his equally skinny assistant tried jacking up the bus with scarce tools, determined with a silent zeal. In Canada the bus would've been steered to a garage, or a change of buses might have taken place. Passenger annoyance couldn't be brooked. But we were in India, and fate governed everything, didn't I know?

"You're in the real India," someone murmured. Professor Lall again?

Getting out the bus, we watched the driver's assistant clamber up the huge, bent back wheel, as if climbing up the Aravelli Hills. With long pliers, a hammer, then an assortment of other tools borrowed from the nearest village to put things straight, the driver figured the bus would soon be on its way. It didn't matter if another hour went by.

I followed Lall around with a new-found resignation, because we knew we couldn't offer much assistance; and vaguely I conjured up tigers once more prowling. Next I dwelled on what Lall had said: "This region has the most unique people in the world living here. Alexander the Great had passed through here, see."

I waited to hear more. "Alexander the Great met people in India he'd never seen anywhere before. His god Hercules didn't prepare him for Indians," Lall impressed upon me. "We're a special people. All your forebears too," he grinned. I smiled at this mild nationalistic boast.

"Selyukas, one of his generals," he added, "remained behind, and settled here. And there was much intermarrying." Did Lall have authentic evidence?

He added, "Now you might see Rajasthani people looking like Europeans, some even have green eyes."

I concentrated on the driver and his assistant working on the back wheel like deranged fanatics. "Yes-yes." Lall wanted to tell me more: the moment was ripe for it because he sensed the writer's instinct in me; and now I must know everything about the history of India, not just about the Mogul past and the Taj Mahal in Agra a couple of hundred miles away. And back in a Delhi side street, hadn't I seen an almost red-haired man with pale skin and almost green eyes? Aryan or European? "We're all Indians," someone had muttered, looking me up and down.

Yes, people with green eyes I would start looking for, wouldn't I?

Lall next talked about the icon of the horse—Shimla—also seen in this region; and India was indeed "God's plenty," meaning it was a land of endless variety. "Paradox is everywhere," he added. "The rich and poor, Brahmin and other castes, and untouchables, all coexisting now. It's no longer a case of a Brahmin hurrying to the opposite side of the street if he saw an untouchable!" He left it at that and grinned. I was eager to hear about the Dalits. But maybe later.

After moments of silence in the balmy night air, with lights flickering in village stalls everywhere before us, I no longer thought of Rajasthan as largely a desert, but with large tracts of land being irrigated where farmers grew abundant wheat. Odd, I immediately thought of the Canadian prairies, too: the heartland.

"Lots of camels are here, you see," Lall said, "because it's a huge desert." He figured maybe I'd be interested in camels. Would I write about camels one day? A vison of camels moving across the Canadian prairie also gripped me. "What do the camels eat?" I asked.

"Greens, such as cauliflower; and kweker, a tough bramble, and neem leaves too," he said. Neem leaves were known to have antiseptic qualities and were used for brushing teeth, "a fact well known," Lall gesticulated for emphasis.

We moved around the bus, as I kept following Lall and other passengers because we had time on our hands. The village was indeed a commercial hive of activity, with everyone selling something or the other, yet no one was buying. In dim light I sauntered, looking around for Alexander's men among the locals, green-eyed people. A solitary man in his twenties sat hunched behind a zinc sheet pulled over a narrow table, a seller of paan: betel leaves chewed by Indians to aid digestion, especially after a sumptuous meal, I'd been told.

With Lall in tow, I approached the stall. Paan was also used to sweeten the breath, Lall explained. The paan-seller's enterprise was rudimentary at best, I noted. "You could become easily addicted to paan," my host murmured, eager to explain it all to me.

Then Lall watched me begin to badger the paan-seller with questions: my sudden interest in his life, all the details. The quiet, pious-looking youth—the seller—said he sat behind his counter from eight in the morning to ten at night. Professor Lall kept translating.

"Is it boring to be here for so many hours?"

"At first it was, but I soon got used to it." The seller's voice was low, barely audible. I imagined him a devotee, not a businessman.

"How much paan do you sell a day?"

"About fifty to a hundred-rupees' worth." In Canadian dollars, about three or four, I calculated. He paid rent to a local outfit, about one hundred rupees a week.

"Are you married?" I tried.

"No," he fluttered a smile. He lived with his mother; his father had died a long time ago. His paan-selling business, meagre, supported him and his mother, and he seemed quietly content with this. He didn't look me in the eye now, as he remained half couched, bowed, maybe because of the weight of his paan-selling business.

I became more curious. "When do you go home to eat?"

He said he left his shop for about an hour each day to do this. I imagined a small, ramshackle place where his mother made chapatis; he would eat two or three, with dhal and curried vegetables, a perfect vegetarian combination. He looked reasonably intelligent, though a far cry from a head of a multinational corporation, if only Indian-style. Did he have ambition of one day maybe living in Delhi and owning a business in Connaught Place—one of the busiest shopping areas in India? Ah, such ambition, dreams!

His eyes flickered. But I knew he was content being a paan-seller; and Lall explained that many of the poor were his customers. "Indians chew paan mixed with tobacco to kill their hunger, you know," he hummed. "It's our way of life."

The bus was still being fixed. A few customers drifted by, chatting, and a sale was made. Paan being chewed the way a cow chewed its cud, I contemplated. The paan-seller again glanced at me, now curious because of the questions. And why didn't I speak Hindi?

Lall made an audible noise about my coming from Canada.

The paan-seller's eyebrows quickly raised.

Would Lall say next that I was a writer and was here to attend a short-story seminar?

The bus was ready to move on, and back in my seat I tried to focus on the seminar ahead: what I'd say about Canada, and also how I would be greeted in Jaipur. Meeting the paan-seller oddly made me feel less anxious; I was starting to feel like an insider now.

I looked back, expecting to see the paan-seller nod as he remained hunched over his stock of betel leaves: like sustained penance while contemplating Brahma, Vishnu, and Shiva, the triumvirate of Hindu gods. His humility and reverence, all that life had stored up for him, mixed with acceptance and the sense of forgiveness too.

The bus's jangly noise prevented me from dwelling on this thought.

Lall chatted with others going to the seminar, and I learnt that there would be an acclaimed writer from Delhi—he, the real insider —as I was yet the Canadian outsider. But there was also intrigue about me, because of my background.

Lall, becoming more affable, carried on, until we arrived in Jaipur about three hours later. And in passing he said we should have taken the train instead: the reputable Shatabdi. But, he quickly added, he wanted to show me the real India. Oh?

In the dining hall at the University of Rajasthan's residence, I watched other guests also attending the seminar wolf down the fare of dhal, vegetable curry, and chapatis. No mutton curry here: vegetarian food was for all palates. And I began to realize that the seminar was a bigger event than I thought.

Contemplatively I ate. Lall encouraged me to eat more, sensing that I was feeling self-conscious. Then he casually said I would soon meet the other keynote speaker: the short-story writer from Delhi, who'd indeed come by train, the Shatabdi. He was a regular at events like these, he hinted. Did the Delhi writer have an inner knowledge of the workings of fate: somehow knowing that the bus would break down?

I asked about the sleeping quarters, and he said the rooms here were the best. "Go there," he pointed, with darkness closing in. A peacock skirted about the lawn outside. My room was on the ground floor, easy to find, Lall indicated. He and the other guests would share rooms on the second and third floors, to save on cost. As a Canadian, I was given the best! I dangled in my hand a long iron key attached to a piece of board, handed to me for my room: this way the key wouldn't get lost, though I needed an extra pocket for it.

I followed the strutting peacock in the swathe of darkness, wondering about the other writer already in his separate room, maybe not far from mine; and he might be contemplating the story he planned to read the next day.

I also needed to rest; I was tired more than I wanted to be because of the long bus ride. Yet unconsciously I began thinking of tigers, then monkeys—one of which had earlier that day snarled at me, ready to scratch my face. The Rajasthan night air I inhaled, and that hut I'd seen on the way, returned, a sustained image, with mythology creeping in around me.

When I thought I'd reached my room I fumbled with the key, in the darkness, pulling open the screen door . . . figuring it was mine. The inside door didn't budge; the key didn't turn.

A grunt from someone inside. A shadowy face peeked out, almost European-looking. A descendant of Alexander? "Pardon me," I quickly said.

I retreated to the dining-room area, but no one was there. Then I hurried back to find my room before it became blacker. Tigers. Monkeys. I struggled with the door. "You . . . again?"

I cursed my mistake a second time. The sadhu-inhabited forest materializing before me, and the Bengal tiger. I figured the guest writer from Delhi occupied the room I tried to enter by mistake.

Finally I found my room. The bed was narrow: the narrowest bed I would ever sleep in. The bathroom area was large. By pulling a long chain, the toilet flushed. Another chain, just a slight jerk, and water poured out.

I reclined on the bed, vaguely looking around for insects. Pigeons on the window sill kept up a sustained badgering . . . all here with a Rajput presence—from a time long ago, India's history flashing before me. And the paan-seller's patient spirit also, with Lall still telling me not to worry. Yes, I would sleep peacefully.

But I concentrated on my speech to be given at the seminar beginning the next morning. And the Delhi writer next door, everything seeming auspicious . . . And I was far away from Canada.

*

Early the next morning the seminar host, effortlessly charming in her elegant sari, welcomed me to the University. She had written scholarly works on feminism in the Indian novel and was highly respected. She wanted to personally "prepare" me for the day's event. Yes, I'd read a story describing my Indian past, the Indian diaspora. Copies of my story, one I'd written about ten years ago, were made: to be discussed by the seminar participants. It would be the same for the Delhi guest writer no doubt—he a descendant of Alexander the Great, in my mind: he might describe what happened when the Greeks first came to India hundreds of years ago!

Microphones aptly placed in the Conference hall, with the scholars—including Professor Lall—all ready to participate. We would hear academic papers on Alice Munro, Margaret Atwood, and other Canadian writers. Commentary about "ethnic" Canadians, such as

Rohinton Mistry and one or two others who wrote about Indian life in East Africa came up. Relationships with Africans in M G Vassanji's novels were echoed, and the term "gunny sack" was used about Indians internalizing European attitudes in their treatment of Africans. Someone shot back that the opposite occurred in the Caribbean, and the term "Anglo-Blackson" was used.

Frowns, everywhere. Next one scholar gave a paper on lesbian Canadian writers, none of whom I had heard about before. Professor Chandra from Varanasi smiled continually as he discussed this subject; and he intended to interview lesbian writers in Canada, and I must make key contacts for him in Montreal, Toronto, Vancouver. Later he would tell me about his difficult life as a child labourer: being light skinned he had no business working in a factory, he chortled. His Brahmin caste didn't help him very much. He said this as if he'd enjoyed being a child labourer.

One scholar from Jawaharlal Nehru University loudly wondered why Alice Munro didn't reflect the changing population of Canada: the many diverse peoples and their religions he'd experienced when he visited Toronto and Vancouver. Why did she write only about people living in small Ontario towns and avoided themes like prejudice, racism, and immigration? A heated discussion followed about a changing Canadian culture, and the word "bogus" was used, alluding to some writers who were real Canadians and others who weren't. And did I stand somewhere in between, an outsider: in Canada or in India? I wrestled with my feelings.

Someone argued that no one must prescribe what a writer should write about. The creative act had to do with freedom! A Maharashtrian from Bombay—a wisp of a woman—arguing this point, said she herself was a closet writer. Her frail hands fluttered.

Another focused on racial tension in the Caribbean immigrant writers; and another quoted V S Naipaul. But Naipaul wasn't Canadian, our charming host interjected. What about racial attitudes held by Indians in the Caribbean: in Trinidad, for instance? Canada seemed forgotten for a while.

My own history and origins I kept thinking about, feeling simultaneously as if my roots were firmly placed elsewhere. But I had to keep in my mind that I was a Canadian.

The sari-clad scholars, many whom I'd seen earlier riding expertly on motor scooters, grew more articulate (I'd vaguely imagined them riding Harley-Davidsons like members of the Montreal's Hell's Angels, one at the head looking like the Dalit Bandit Queen, Phoolan Devi). The paan-seller also wasn't far from my mind, and the sadhu in his forest hut with the tiger approaching in saffron light glowing. And Canada . . . a far land, the more I listened to speaker after speaker.

Professor Lall kept gauging my mood, my reaction, I sensed. He detected torture in my soul, he would later tell me. And the other guest writer from Delhi was somewhere in the audience, no doubt looking at me. And last night I had disturbed his sleep, all in my indubitable Canadian manner. Was I still longing for insider status?

My turn at the podium: the occasion it seemed many were waiting for—the Canadian that I was, but an immigrant also, with diaspora intact. I read my story "Rivers and Trees," contriving resonance in my voice, as I recreated the life of an indentured immigrant in faraway South America, where I was born. Catapulted back in time and space I was, as if I was the last of the line separated from my Uttar Pradesh forebears. Loud moans I heard, coming from the women scholars who'd earlier used mind-boggling terms, in their intellectual "discourse."

Lall was pleased, I could tell. The applause was led by him.

Then the Delhi guest writer's turn, whose door I had knocked on last night. Fate indeed bringing us together, I surmised; and the image of his being descended from Alexander, too. Daruwalla, tallish, a figure well cut, in his late fifties: he was calm as he read his story, one that kept becoming more textured as he read, myths and beliefs all finely embedded in his words. The central character's name was Goberdhan, and I recalled an uncle by that name when I was growing up.

Now here in Jaipur, echoes of Goberdhan seemed all.

I listened to the Delhi writer as I listened to no other in Canada. After the applause, I went up to him and told him I thought that he might be a descendant of one of Alexander's generals. He smiled, and muttered that he saw symbolism in what I said. He indicated that he was a Parsi, and I nodded. Was he also an outsider and did I have something in common with him?

With our charming hostess looking on, I again apologized for disturbing him last night. He said he'd been putting the final touches to his story. Lall, next to us, asked if I'd done the same with my story last night: the central character being an old man chopping down a solid tree similar to the banyan, and the wayward village youths laughing at him. The Delhi writer agreed that my central character might be an outsider, being far from India.

I struggled with the idea of this character also coming from Canada, I said. Yes, diaspora was at the heart of everything I wrote, all agreed.

From among a knot of sari-clad women scholars, a shy young female student came forward, giving me a small present: something wrapped in shiny silk paper. She was pleased to meet me, she said. She had heard a lot about Canada and hoped to come there one day, maybe to visit me . . . and even to find out why so many Indians wanted to come to Canada. It would be her future study. Everyone laughed. I also laughed.

More of the seminar participants from Kanpur, Madras, Kerala, Shimla, shook hands with me, one calling me a long-lost brother. Our host kept smiling. Maybe it was what I needed to feel to be a real writer.

Professor Lall murmured, words sounding like I shouldn't forget the paan-seller also: as if he'd organized things in such a manner . . . including for the bus to have a flat on the way so I would meet the paan-seller. Everything was ordained, didn't I know?

Before I could dwell more on this, the young female student asked why I really lived in Canada: and what I tried to explore in my work.

Our host quietly said, "Fiction has many lives," sounding prophetic. I shrugged, I wasn't sure.

The gift in my hand, neatly wrapped with silk cloth and fine-textured paper. I wasn't sure what was inside.

Daruwalla smiled and vaguely muttered to himself about the short story not being like a "sari displayed to eager women shoppers."

Later when I returned to my room, I slowly opened the small present, carefully unwrapping the silk paper.

The bronze image of an elephant, the god Ganesha, was in my hand.

It also looked somewhat like a bear. Ganesha was the deity of strength and learning. Oddly, I also thought of the bear in the sky, the native's own, with the Great Spirt, somewhere intact. I puzzled over this for a while, as I'd puzzled with my own emotion, feelings. And the more I considered it, the more I felt I was now an insider, with the paan-seller's face coming back to me: all his reverence or piety sitting before his stall from morning to night.

Then the noise of the bus trundling along, on our return to Delhi, now by train, the Shatabdi. And I kept thinking of the elephant all the while, the insider that I was.

Professor Lall hummed, "You see . . . ?"

"See?"

He grinned.

Yes, the sensations I'd recorded, all that I experienced . . . and looking at the Aravelli Hills, the oldest in India, and thinking of a far past, or a close-up present, which I would be taking back to Canada. And the image of Alexander the Great rolling across these same hills, and then being unable to go further in his quest to conquer the world. Strangely, I began imagining too having green or blue eyes because of my having come from the land of my ancestors and living in Canada all these years. The Delhi writer smiling. The god Ganesha in my hand, as I again contemplated the bear in the sky . . . when I returned home.

# Siddhartha

In my small village in South America, in that country, I was struggling to be a writer. I wanted to see my name in print, and maybe become famous one day: a thrill I looked forward to, young as I was; then everyone would look up to me. And it was also the sense of being in the same league as the likes of Dickens, Shakespeare, T S Eliot, Walt Whitman. Thus my wishful thinking, or sheer self-indulgence, as daily I wrote on my small Hermes manual typewriter in the tropical heat. Then the trade winds would blow, tempering the heat, as I breathed in hard, inhaling sugar-cane smells everywhere: a plantation world indeed. At nights, I wrote poems, images drawn from the past: ghosts of lives lived, mixed with images of the present, the imagination being all. I would win international awards, I figured; and hadn't I already won a gold medal, seeing it as a symbol of my life's work to come? I recreated in my mind the image of myself going up a large hall in the capital city to receive my medal, as everyone gasped: "He's just a young boy!" With the medal pinned on my tight jacket, I was convinced more than ever that I was a writer!

Now I wanted to be published abroad, in England or America. The latter seemed more exciting, the great big country where writers everywhere wanted to be: where Hemingway had come from; and indeed I wanted to be published by the *New Yorker* and *Harper's* and other famous magazines, which I'd sometimes see on the racks of the best bookstore in the nearby town. I also imagined a great big publisher in New York City like Random House reading my manuscript and becoming excited by what I wrote: my sheaf of poems—their eagerly reading it and being amazed by what I thought in distant South America. Ah, I was a gold medallist, remember! Now I would explore new avenues of thought, human existence, unfamiliar in America and Europe.

Every other day I would go to the main library in the town and read zealously, and imagine. I wanted to pattern myself after so many English and American writers, all whom I read, and each time I visualized my name in print. Once in a while I also imagined myself a journalist. But it was a writer of books I wanted to be, to explore the depths of human emotions, nothing less. I imagined actually going to New York City and presenting myself in person, after my book of poems had been published by them. Yes, I was the famous writer they'd been corresponding with for years. My fantasy ongoing. But I was still here, the heat more intense, though the trade winds kept blowing. Weeks, months going by.

Finally I had enough poems, my best, all selected carefully; my emotion in them was sometimes overwrought, yet there was strong, bold imagery mixed with the sense of dream, everything occurring in a faraway place, and soon leading me into a bigger, changing world. And America's hippie movement I conjured up: long-haired young people everywhere, all wanting change! The sixties it was, and a Black Power movement was also what I heard about and lived for on the radio: the genuine protests, and fire, bombing, looting. And many young white people too wanted change! As a writer in a faraway place I kept wanting to be aware of everything going on, seeing it all clearly from my vantage point. Yes, it was my business to know everything, and eventually I would put my village on the world map because of my collection of poems.

I was still glued to my radio (there was no TV) in my room, with the door bolted, as I kept concentrating. And once in a while I actually imagined wearing a zoot suit, flaunting myself, being far out! I contemplated other exciting events too occurring in America, and then a man landing on the moon. But reality suddenly brought me back home: the sugar plantation world, all in the midst of exploitation and oppression. Well, I didn't exactly call it that; and cane fires kept rising, ready to start the new harvest season. The giant cane factory throbbing all around, with the youths and older people working in the cane fields, and I'd written about them in sharp, clear images in my poems. This consciousness beating in me.

Indeed I kept thinking of the only publisher I wanted . . . in New York, Random House, the only one I knew about. No thought of first getting my poems published in the small literary magazines; and I saw little if any of the small magazines. I figured I was a gold medallist, and the great big New York publisher would be interested in me.

With manuscript neatly tucked in a brown envelope, I went to our local post office on my bicycle. The postmaster smiled at me, as if he had an inkling of what I was about. He knew of my interests, that I wanted to be a famous writer. "You sure?" the bespectacled man grinned.

"Sure?" I pretended not to understand him.

He laughed as he handed me the stamps after weighing the parcel.

My handwriting, crisp, neat, the address written clearly on the envelope; the poems now being sent to Random House in New York. And a whole week's savings used to buy the stamps. But I thought nothing of it: the poems were going to America to be published—I wanted to declare to the postmaster with a small boast.

The heat everywhere interminable, almost blazing; the silk cotton and poinsettia trees by the roadside next to the black sage shrubs and starfruit like sorrel withering. And monkey-apple shrubs, sometimes full blown in the intermittent trade wind, alongside guava and jamun. Birds, the blue-sackie and yellow-breasted kiskadee twittering. Em-

erald-looking hummingbirds zoomed left and right, sometimes whirring in the air, a miracle before the eyes. Dragonflies, long winged,
incessantly flitted about. I stretched out my index finger and thumb
against the glass window of our house and tried holding one dragon-
fly . . . wingless, yet it fluttered away! Images I contrived in my poems . . . including strands of burnt cane leaves floating in the air like
tarantula, then falling everywhere after another fire, all in the continuing harvest season.

My poems being read in New York. Where else? At night my
thoughts festering, dreams becoming nightmares. Then like a salve, I
again thought of the editors, who knew the world's literature, now being amazed by what I wrote. And soon they'd send me a letter, saying
they had agreed to publish my poems. I would make my mark.

Three weeks passed, then a month; two months, then almost three.
New York was taking a long time to reply because the editors were
deliberating over each of my poems, and indeed considering how best
to publish them in book form, and for it eventually to reach a big,
wide audience. Then the worrisome thought that maybe my manuscript was lost in New York: the great big metropolis! It'd be the end
of all I had dreamt about, though I had made a vague carbon copy,
smudged in places; and how I wished that my poems were safe, and
were being read.

I would look expectantly at the postman coming down the street,
hoping he would hand me a letter from New York saying that my poems were accepted.

He smiled, passed by.

The next day again, and the next, same thing.

Then one day he stopped and handed me a large brown parcel. My
poems? He smiled, and rode on. And indeed my poems were returned, from New York: Random House itself, all in an offi-
cial-looking parcel. And it was large, as I figured they'd commented
on each poem, line by line. I would benefit from such a rejection slip!

Carefully I opened the large parcel.

In it were my poems, returned with a curt rejection slip; but there was another sheaf of poems neatly tied, with a rejection slip attached, all in the same envelope. The other poet was from Illinois. Random House had mistakenly put both rejected manuscripts in the same envelope . . . and mailed it to me all the way in South America! The blow of my rejection wasn't bad anymore; at least an American was also rejected.

Eagerly I read the other poet's work; his name was Burrows, with the initials A M in front. And his poems were all serious, filled with an intense pain; a great, huge sadness. Line after line, the same mood, feeling, without coming to an end. I was perplexed, wondering why in America, the richest country in the world, was there such sadness. I became absorbed in the poet's deep, inner pain, Rilke-like, with a touch of Emily Dickinson: little that I knew of both poets' works; and I thought that maybe the turmoil America was going through might have affected his spirit; and the war in Vietnam also, with the many veterans, some to become homeless people and hanging out in American streets with a limb missing and asking for help. This pain came to me all the way in my village.

I read the poems again, as I figured Burrows wanted me to; and maybe he was still waiting to hear back from Random House, rejection slip and all. Finally I wrote to him, explaining to him what had happened.

In two weeks, I received a reply; he was pleased that his poems were in my hands, he said, and he wanted me to keep the poems: he had copies of them—and now I should send him some of mine. But his poems intimidated me because of their intensity, and I didn't send him any of mine.

Instead I carefully copied in long hand the best known of our local poets (their few books weren't available in America, I knew) and sent them to him. A poet named Wilson Harris he should look out for. And another, named Martin Carter.

In no time he wrote back, and always there was his pain, the blood of ink, all his heart's outpouring. This time he sent me a book by Herman Hesse, *Siddhartha,* saying I should read it.

I kept wondering what kind of name Burrows was: if he was of African or European descent. But he wanted me to read about Siddhartha; maybe he figured I was of Indian background. Yes, I would be interested in some kind of holiness, a life of reverence. A life of contemplation too while longing for bliss, and shunning materialistic things. The cane factory still pounding.

Yet I kept thinking of his pain living in America. And Siddhartha's world, the spiritual path, mysticism and seeking salvation, all that he might be after. Herman Hesse no doubt was a fad in America, I began to think, on all the university and college campuses, among beatniks everywhere: the same who fought the establishment with sit-ins, demonstrations. All searching for spiritual truth, some even quoting Krishnamurti's "every leaf must first be green." Burrows writing it all in long, copious letters, which he sent to me in South America.

Other spiritual paths being pursued, with gurus from India, I imagined also. And there was a famous Indian poet named Rabindranath Tagore, a Bengali, much revered. Did Burrows know about him? Some of the locals would quote from Tagore, amazing me.

But Burrows wasn't too interested in Tagore, I sensed. And his first name was Michael, and for him it was only *Siddhartha* by Herman Hesse. Now my own Hindu family background I contemplated, looking at Hesse's novel afresh. I wrote and told Burrows this, what I thought about where my ancestors had come from in India, long ago. I wrote too about my mother's faith, her devotion to God. Then I tore up the letter. Instead I read *Siddhartha* again, page after page, contemplating Buddha's life, and the quest for nirvana. And I no longer looked at the workers around me; I merely thought of life and a denial of the senses as the essence of finding spiritual salvation.

My mother was taken aback by what I started saying to her. Other family members also, some looking at me askance, then with amusement, tittering. The young cane workers snickered, and I wanted to show them the American's letter. And why didn't Burrows write something about Martin Luther King, Jr, or about the Black Power movement and the Black Panthers, and about Stokely Carmichael,

Malcolm X, Eldridge Cleaver, all whom I wanted to hear about from him, first hand? It was only about his angst, as he called it, sheer pain. I kept wondering what kind of American he was.

Next I tried to imagine the many ethnic groups in America: Irish, German, Norwegian, Native, all amidst the more plentiful Anglo-Saxon population, descendants of the same who'd first arrived at Plymouth Harbour on the Mayflower in 1620. Of course, I thought too of the period of slavery, and the American Civil War. And about the Boston Tea Party. Next I wondered if Burrows was his real name, or a made-up one. Could he be writing under a pseudonym? No, he wouldn't be.

On the newscast more demonstrations occurring in America, and fires raging, as I heard someone call America a "sick society," especially when President Kennedy was shot. And the war in Vietnam, in all of South East Asia. Then Martin Luther King was shot. And Bobby Kennedy was shot, too. Who was Lee Harvey Oswald? Who, Sirhan Sirhan? Who the Mafia?

Resonances of Castro and a Bay of Pigs invasion. The CIA, and the ongoing Cold War, with the Russian threat of spreading Marxism-Leninism everywhere in South and Central America. Yet the poet from Illinois kept writing to me, only about his personal pain.

The Buddhist life he contemplated on, and I was slowly doing the same, not seeking after material things, but wanting to achieve bliss only, nirvana. Hesse's writing seemed so effortless, as if I was dipping into the water of life in a lily pond, with lotus leaves hardly creating a ripple. Flowers on long stalks, pendulous, all around. An image of the Ganges too I conjured up, and my being in Benares (or somewhere like it), and sitting under a huge banyan tree. Dharma, the rule of life, and the Eightfold Path to live by, and going through the cycle of life and death, and rebirth. Such karma. "The disciples of Gautama are ever awake and watchful, and their minds day and night ever delight in compassion," the American wrote. These words I reflected on, Siddharta's own.

My being in Benares, the holiest of cities, not far from where my forebears had come from, I thought; then Bihar, with Bodh Gaya. More letters, books exchanged, and I wasn't preoccupied with becoming famous anymore, or writing new poems for that matter. All the while the cane factory kept throbbing. And those around me asked what was the matter. The postman also asked, "What's with you, Boy?"

"Nothing," I said.

"Ah, he's influenced by all the new books he's been reading from America."

"Am I?" I smiled and left it at that, still seeking after the spiritual path.

One night in my room, all alone, I imagined meeting Burrows in America, with all his pain, and we would together share blissful thoughts, begin a healing too.

Did he want that? Next I imagined him coming to visit me in South America, in my village. He, in a long flowing white robe, something like that. No, I preferred going to America, I thought. Maybe I'd drop by at Random House in New York with him, the two of us together.

I smiled. Did he also smile?

"What's he thinking?" the villagers asked. My mother, a diehard Hindu as she was known to be, hummed an answer, as if she indeed knew. "It's his writing, his poetry," someone muttered. "He's received a rejection slip from America already. He should give it up."

"Give what up?" asked others, laughing.

Faintly I nodded to them. And I continued with the life of denial of the senses, sometimes going without food for a day or two at a time, like Buddha, and thinking of goodness and virtue. And maybe, in America I'd find true bliss. Soon. Not in Benares, but in Chicago, Illinois, or in some other city close by. I'd go on a pilgrimage also, before long. I imagined Burrows waving to me, distantly, then close up.

Other writers and poets, all coming with me too, seeking a combination of art and holiness. It was such a time to be in America, despite fires raging, looting, and police beatings. Next, shootings at Kent State University; and no psychedelic drugs we'd need, no marijuana or other forms of dope. Yes, every leaf must first be green as Krishnamurti said—the Illinois poet reminding everyone. Maybe he was black, an African American, I thought. Now Random House and other publishers would finally join us, all in one big happy family, protesting. Perhaps.

*

I arrived in North America, for the first time, and found myself in Northern Ontario, the closest to America I'd be, for now maybe. And over time, the path I'd set for myself slowly began to disappear. It was amazing how this started happening.

Yet I fought to regain the past, each hour of the day, imagining myself a fanatic. I kept wanting to be a writer, as if to reinstate something in me. I read magazines from all parts of the world, though mainly from Canada, the USA, Australia, the UK, and dwelled on what the many poets wrote about, what everyone's expectations and ambitions were. And the open, unabashed attitude to sex, I thought about, puritanical as I might have been. But none seemed to be like the Illinois poet, who for some strange reason no longer wrote to me. Was it because he realized I'd come to North America?

I kept thinking of him as my "friend," and read more of Herman Hesse's books in the local university library, and read also the beat generation writers like Kerouac and Ferlinghetti, and others from Los Angeles and New York, including someone who wrote a long poem called "Howl." Allen Ginsberg was his name. Despite all this, it was the Illinois poet's angst that stayed with me, his manuscript that had come all the way to me in my village in South America that I'd dragged along.

I also took part in sit-ins, remaining rigid before the university president's office. I chatted with activist Jane Fonda (if only briefly) when she visited, a firebrand as she was, condemning the Vietnam War; and with other voices I kept shouting for change, and maybe I no longer wanted to find bliss anymore.

An intense lifestyle; and presidents being rallied against: Lyndon Johnson, Richard Nixon. Existentialism in the air, my very own. I

was starting to understand the American poet, my friend, finally.
I also wore faded blue jeans with patches on it. Voices exclaiming,
"Peace, man!" Yes, peace . . . and nirvana, I hoped. From time to
time, I thought of my mother back in the village, her own Hindu
mantras being chanted. And the Illinois poet gradually started disappearing from my consciousness. It was strange how this started happening.

My mother's image, sustained: she, still chanting in her pujas, her
eyes closed, incense reeking, ghee acrid, becoming overpowering as
smoke swirled. The fire of purification. Thinking of eternity too, I
was, and maybe life's fuller meaning, having faith in God. All things
transcendental. Again I heard, "Peace, man!"

Time evanescent, everything passing us by, as I decided to write
more poems: now about life in Northern Ontario and experiencing
winds howling like an elephant in distress.

*Edmund Fitzgerald* going under in Lake Superior, and Gordon
Lightfoot's requiem, an image not unlike the *Titanic* sinking off the
coast of Newfoundland. Yes, some of it contrived. And Anne Murray
singing her ballads, and the poets Leonard Cohen and Irving Layton
in Montreal, and so many others in Toronto, including a woman
named Margaret Atwood. All I became enthusiastic about.

But it was still the poet from Illinois, with his deep pain, assuaged
by the images of Siddhartha, who kept coming back to me. "How is
it?" Canadians asked me. Did they mean my search for truth and nirvana? Or did they mean the quest to become famous?

I shook my head. "How about the American you're looking for,
have you met him finally?"

They figured it was only because of him I'd come to live in North
America. And somewhere a voice in the village, back there, kept asking, "Come on, what's he really like?"

I visualized him wearing faded blue jeans with a thousand patches
on it; and maybe he'd be long haired, his face haggard-looking, yet
soulful, but carrying his deep inner sadness; all of which seemed to
go beyond the campus sit-ins with others, humming along with John

Lennon and Bob Dylan. My mother I sensed next looking at me, and she understood me right then. She knew about my striving for nirvana, all that one experienced through karma. And maybe after denying the life of the senses, transcendence would be close by.

Vaguely I again thought of the poet from Illinois, still going through the long period of angst, his travail and suffering interminable: like America's own sickness.

And when we'd finally meet, I imagined him saying, "See, it had to be so."

"What d'you mean?"

"It's because of Siddhartha, my friend," he calmly said.

Oddly, I was glad he said that, as I kept looking at him: the transformed figure reading his poems to me.

Time yet evanescent, passing us by.

"No, no," he finally said. "No more, I can't bear it much longer."

I was never able to find out what he couldn't bear much longer.

Then he disappeared. And it was as if he'd never appeared in my life, as I kept on writing my poems, each word, image, carefully carved. Each phase, line, stanza. And somewhere they were looking at me, from back there. Looking at me hard, one or two frowning, and wondering about my life, asking my mother . . . what had become of me.

They kept asking. And I never wanted to return, despite trade winds, and the cane fields burning, with strands floating in the air. And somewhere my mother kept hailing me, as if only she understood my yearning for peace and bliss—in a time yet to come.